The Island Murders

Rachel McLean writes thrillers that make your pulse race and your brain tick. Originally a self-publishing sensation, she has sold millions of copies digitally, with massive success in the UK, and a growing reach internationally too. She is also the author of the Detective Zoe Finch series, which precedes the Dorset Crime novels, and the spin-off McBride & Tanner series and Cumbria Crime series. In 2021 she won the Kindle Storyteller Award with *The Corfe Castle Murders* and her last five books have all hit No1 in the Bookstat ebook chart on launch.

Also by Rachel McLean

Dorset Crime series

The Corfe Castle Murders
The Clifftop Murders
The Island Murders

RACHEL McLEAN

THE ISLAND MURDERS

hera

First published in Ackroyd Publishing in 2021 by the United Kingdom

This edition published in the United Kingdom in 2024 by

Hera Books
Unit 9 (Canelo), 5th Floor
Cargo Works, 1-2 Hatfields
London SE1 9PG
United Kingdom

A CIP catalogue record for this book is available from the British Library.

Print ISBN 978 1 80436 762 9

Look for more great books at www.herabooks.com

Printed and bound in Great Britain by Clays Ltd, Elcograf S.p.A.

CHAPTER ONE

Frankie knocked on the door of the low-roofed cottage and pulled her arms around herself, wishing she'd brought a jacket. She caught movement out of the corner of her eye and turned to see a rabbit disappearing around the side of the building. She smiled. Rabbits got the visitors excited, but they were as common as rats on Brownsea Island. Red squirrels: now they were more of a rarity. The visitors came here every day, seeking them out, marvelling over their rareness. What they didn't know was that once the visitors had gone home, the squirrels came out to play. Walk through the woods on an early morning or an evening, and there were plenty of them leaping between the trees.

The door opened and Frankie pulled on a smile. Natasha was her line manager, a good one, if a little distant at times. More distant recently.

Frankie would have preferred not to have the team meeting at Natasha's house. But by 8pm on a Tuesday, all the visitors gone, the island had been closed for the evening, and inspections were complete. The public buildings were closed, and there was nowhere else to meet.

Of course, there were plenty of suitable rooms in the so-called castle. But those were reserved for the John

Lewis staff. The National Trust team had to make do with what they could get.

Frankie followed Natasha through the narrow hall. A door was closed on the left-hand side and Frankie could hear a TV beyond it. That would be Bernard, Natasha's husband. She could just about make out the sound of the news. She followed Natasha through to the kitchen to find Anya already there, her fingers wrapped around a mug of coffee. Anya glanced up, her eyes looking tired.

"Hi, Frankie."

"Hey, Anya." Frankie took a seat opposite her.

Natasha flicked on the kettle. "What can I get you Frankie? Tea, coffee, wine?"

Frankie eyed Natasha's glass, sitting on the table half full of red wine. She shook her head. "Coffee for me, please."

It might be OK for the team leader to drink during team meetings, but she preferred to keep her wits about her. Natasha rattled around while Frankie made herself comfortable. The table in the centre of Natasha's kitchen was old, made of rough pine with mismatched chairs surrounding it. Every time she came here, she had to turn her chair a few degrees to stop it from moving up and down on the tiles. Anya smiled as she watched Frankie making herself comfortable.

"Good day?" Anya asked.

Frankie shrugged. "Northern hide was busy today, plenty of birds."

Anya took a sip of her coffee. "Squirrels are busy too. I think we might have a nest up by Rough Brake."

"Nice," said Frankie, "The tourists will like that."

Anya laughed. "So will I."

Frankie checked her watch. Quarter past seven. She looked up at Natasha. "No Simone?"

Natasha didn't turn from her position at the kettle. "She called in sick."

Simone lived next door to Frankie in a building on the north of the island. It was handy for the lagoon and the birds that Frankie liked to watch over.

"You should have told me," she said. "I would have popped in to check on her."

Natasha turned and placed a cup of coffee on the table. "Sorry, I've been busy. Head office has got some new schemes they want us to try out."

The door opened behind Frankie, and Bernard entered. He was a few years older than Natasha, and significantly taller.

He rubbed at the stubble on his chin and yawned. "Evening ladies," he said.

Frankie stiffened and nodded.

Anya gave him a wide smile. "Evening, Bernard."

He smiled back at her, his eyes glistening. He went over to the sink and put his arms around his wife. "Hello gorgeous," he said.

She turned to him. "Hi, you."

He burrowed his face into her neck and inhaled her scent. She shivered as he did so.

Frankie watched all this. Bernard liked to demonstrate possession of his wife when other people were in the house. He liked to put his hands on her and remind them that despite the fact that she was one of the most senior members of the team here, and he was just a lowly free-lance journalist, she was still his wife. He rubbed Natasha on the top of the head, like she was a dog. Not caring that her hair got messed up. She frowned but didn't raise her hand to straighten it. He pinched her waist, and she laughed and flapped a tea towel at him. Frankie narrowed

3

her eyes. Bernard reminded her of her own ex-husband; he'd been all hands, too.

Bernard looked at Frankie and tipped his fingers to his forehead. "You alright there, Frankie?"

"Fine, thank you, Bernard."

His smile broadened. "I'll leave you ladies to it then."

"See you soon," said Anya.

Frankie grunted. She didn't like the patronising way he called them 'ladies'.

He turned back to his wife and gave her a final kiss which she returned. He left the kitchen and she sat at the table, her cheeks flushed.

"Shouldn't we put this off until Simone is better?" Frankie asked, sipping at her coffee.

Natasha shook her head. "I want to update you on these plans from head office. It will affect the hides, Frankie."

Frankie sighed. She liked her job the way it was, and she knew the wildlife did, too. But head office was head office. They liked to experiment, they liked to try out new ideas.

Two hours later, the meeting finally drew to a close. The plans from head office didn't look like they would go anywhere, and Frankie wasn't about to champion them. She pushed her chair back and made for the door, muttering her farewells to the other two women. She left the house to find a dark figure sitting out front, perched on a wall and swinging his feet.

She approached him. "Are you waiting for me?" she asked.

He grinned, his face dim in the low light from the front windows of the house.

"Fancy a walk home?" he said.

"I'm a big girl," she told him. "I don't need escorting."

He grabbed her around the waist and pulled her into him. She leaned against him, inhaling the warm smell of his fleece.

Adam was still wearing his National Trust fleece, the one he wore all day when he was volunteering.

"You need a bath," she told him.

He laughed and pulled back. "Later," he said. "Let's get down to the beach." He raised an eyebrow.

She yawned. "I'm tired. That meeting, God." She put her hand to her forehead.

Adam gave her a hug. "I know. But it's your dream job, it's worth the occasional hour of admin."

She nodded and looked up at him. They were walking together, heading back towards their house on the north side of the island. Adam was five inches taller than her, and when she looked up at him she could just about make out the moonlight behind him.

"Go on then," she said.

He turned to her and grinned, then pulled on her hand and led her off towards the south of the island where the beaches sloped down to the sea. Their house overlooked the Poole side of the island. If you walked into the woods from their back door, you could see Poole Harbour and the massive ships. But over on this side of the island, where the accessible beaches were, it was completely different. Opposite was the dark shape of the Isle of Purbeck. The hills nothing more than shadows at this time of night.

But Frankie and Adam knew these paths and beaches. They'd lived here for the last year and a half, and it had become as familiar to them as their own skin. They hurried down towards the beach. Frankie shivered, whether from the chill or anticipation she wasn't sure. As they reached the end of the path, Adam let go of her hand and went on ahead. She followed him down the steep steps that led down to a small beach, one of many on this side of the island.

They liked to come here at night, when everybody else was asleep, and the island was quiet. The visitors were gone, the staff were tucked up for the night, and they had the beach and the views to themselves. As they reached the sand, he turned and opened his arms wide, and she ran into them, whooping. He laughed and swung her around. She loved this man. Her relationship with him couldn't be any more different from her first marriage. He plonked her down on the sand and gave her a kiss on the forehead.

"Race you!" he said.

This beach was short, but they liked to run along it kicking up sand as they went. If she was lucky, he might grab her and lead her behind the rocks further up. She felt a chill run through her.

He ran on ahead and then suddenly stopped. She caught up with him and put a hand on his back.

"What is it?" she panted.

He was staring ahead of them, his eyes catching the dim light.

"What is it?" she repeated.

He pointed. "What's that?" he murmured.

She followed his gaze. There was a shape on the sand down by the water's edge, waves washing over it.

"A seal?" she said.

He turned to her. "You don't get seals in Poole Harbour."

She shrugged. "We might get lucky one day."

He shook his head. "That's no seal, it's wearing clothes."

Frankie felt a shiver run across her skin. This time she knew it wasn't anticipation. She swallowed and took a step forward.

Adam put a hand on her arm. "It's okay love. I'll go."

"No," she said, "Don't be ridiculous."

She walked on ahead, pulling in deep breaths. It would be an animal, she told herself. Some driftwood washed up to the beach. It wasn't what she was thinking.

As she approached the shape the trees receded overhead and the light became brighter. She stared at it, her mouth dry.

She put her hand to her chest and turned to her partner. "Adam!" she called. "Adam, come here quickly!"

CHAPTER TWO

Lesley opened and closed the cupboard doors in between scratching an itch on her arm. "Where's the blue mug?" she said. "It's the best one for black coffee."

Elsa smiled as she rose from her spot on her sofa. "It's in the dishwasher. You used it earlier."

Lesley turned to her. She batted at the itch on her arm and slumped against the counter. "Did I?"

"Yes, honey. You want me to get it out for you?"

Lesley eyed the dishwasher. She knew what happened if you opened the door while it was running: a face full of warm water. "No."

She opened the cupboard door again and rooted through the mugs, looking for an alternative.

Elsa came up behind her. She slipped her arms around Lesley's waist. "You've already picked your favourite mug," she said. "It's nice."

Lesley tensed. She'd heard rumours about women doing this. Three dates, and they were hiring a U-HAUL and moving in together. Lesley wasn't even divorced from her unfaithful husband yet. She wasn't ready to start cohabiting.

She pulled her arms in to her sides and stepped out of Elsa's embrace, turning to face her.

"I've got my place in Wareham," she said.

Elsa's dark eyes roamed Lesley's face. "It's OK." She stroked Lesley's cheek. "It's normal to be scared."

"I'm not scared," Lesley said. She was a Detective Chief Inspector. She didn't scare easily.

Elsa raised an eyebrow. "Not that kind of scared. Commitment scared. You've not long come out of your marriage to Terry."

Lesley shrugged her shoulders and reached round for the mug. "I don't want to talk about Terry."

She still hadn't seen him since she'd caught him with his mistress three months earlier. A surprise trip back to Birmingham, and she'd been rewarded by the sight of another woman standing in her kitchen. Wearing Lesley's own dressing gown.

She grabbed a mug, a chipped white one, and slammed it down next to the kettle.

"Hey, calm down," Elsa said. "What's up?"

"Nothing," Lesley replied.

She slopped water into the mug, realising she hadn't put coffee granules in yet. Elsa reached out and moved the mug aside.

"What are you doing?" she said. "Use the machine."

Lesley shook her head. "This is fine. I just want something to keep me awake."

"But it's almost ten o'clock. You'll be buzzing, you won't sleep."

"I've got work to do," Lesley replied, her back still to Elsa. "Paperwork."

"Here?" Elsa asked her.

"No." Lesley turned. "I'll go back to the house."

Elsa frowned. "Your little cottage in Wareham. The one you hate."

Lesley looked at her. "I don't hate it. I'm getting to quite like it, you know."

"The doorways are so low you have to stoop your head when you move around, the TV is about two feet away from the sofa, and as for the kitchen…"

Lesley curled her lip. "Don't knock it," she said. "It's not as bad as you think."

Elsa raised her arms in supplication. "OK, OK. It's your cosy little cottage." She sighed. "Jeez, I didn't know I was getting into this."

"Getting into what?"

Elsa looked into Lesley's eyes, biting her bottom lip. Normally Lesley found it cute when she did this. But tonight…

Lesley watched as Elsa walked into the living room and sat on the sofa. Her flat was on the third floor, just a few streets back from the beach. The kitchen and living room were open plan, with wide windows and low sunshine silhouetting the furniture. She picked up the remote control and started scrolling through Netflix.

"Into what?" Lesley approached the back of the sofa.

Elsa looked up at her, her face dark. "You've been off with me, ever since they arrested Priscilla Evans."

"Priscilla Evans," Lesley said. "What's she got to do with anything?"

Elsa paused the programme she'd picked and dropped the remote in her lap. "Is it because you had to rescue me from her, or because she killed Harry?"

Priscilla Evans had been having an affair with Elsa's business partner Harry Nevin. She'd killed him after discovering he was also seeing a junior partner. At one point, she'd believed him to be in a relationship with Elsa, too.

"No," Lesley said. "It's not that." But it was, at least in part.

Elsa looked away from Lesley. She'd hit play on the programme but wasn't focusing on the screen.

"You've just been weird ever since then." She looked up again at Lesley. "I know Priscilla thought I was shagging Harry, but you didn't, did you?"

"Of course not," said Lesley, her skin bristling.

"So what's up?"

"Nothing," Lesley replied, looking at her mug. She blew on the coffee. She shouldn't have made this, if she was planning to go back to the house. Truth was, she hadn't been planning on doing that until a moment ago.

But she'd been tense since the Nevin case. Lesley had discovered things about Elsa, about the clients she represented. She wasn't sure if Elsa knew that she knew.

She rounded the sofa and sat down next to Elsa, placing a hand on her knee. She rubbed it and Elsa leaned in towards her.

"I'm sorry," Lesley said. "It's just my boss, he's being a dick at the moment."

Elsa laughed. "That's what bosses do. Particularly if you're a copper."

"Yeah," Lesley sighed. "But I need to get going."

"OK. When will I see you again?"

Lesley shrugged. "Tomorrow maybe, day after?"

"Good," said Elsa. She placed her hand over Lesley's, still on her knee. "You're not pissed off with me?"

"No," said Lesley. She could hear tension in her voice.

"Good." Elsa pulled her hand away and stood up. "I'll see you tomorrow, then."

Lesley looked up at her. "I don't get a kiss?"

Elsa leaned over Lesley. She placed her hands on the back of the sofa, either side of Lesley's head. "Of course you get a kiss, honey."

CHAPTER THREE

Frankie hammered on Natasha's door.

"Natasha!" she cried. "Open up!"

Natasha would be getting ready for bed. Bernard wouldn't appreciate being disturbed. But this house was the closest to the beach and they needed help, fast.

Adam ran up behind Frankie, barrelling into the door. It shuddered under his weight.

"Ow!" she cried.

"Sorry," he panted. "Anybody in?"

"Of course they're in," Frankie said. "They'll be going to bed."

She hammered on the door again. This time it opened.

Natasha stood in front of them, light silhouetting her frizzy hair. She still wore makeup on one eye but not the other.

"What is it?" she said, glancing over her shoulder. "Did you forget something?"

Frankie shook her head. Her breathing was shallow.

"No, it's… it's…" She stared at Natasha, the words refusing to come.

"It's Simone," said Adam.

Frankie put a hand out to the doorpost. "We found her."

"What? Where?" asked Natasha.

Frankie felt her legs weaken. She leaned against the doorpost.

"Where?" asked Natasha. Her eyes were wide, her face pale. "Is she OK?"

Frankie shook her head.

Natasha took a step forward, her eyes full of concern. "Is she sick?" she said. "Is it serious? Oh, *shit*." She looked over her shoulder into the house. "Getting paramedics over here takes forever."

Frankie swallowed. "She doesn't need paramedics. At least I…"

"What then?" snapped Natasha. "What's happened?"

"We found her on the beach," said Adam.

Frankie lowered her head, listening to him speak. All she could see was the shape of Simone's body on the beach. Her legs had been tangled in seaweed, and her hair had been matted. How long had she been there? When was it she'd called in sick?

She raised her head and stared at Natasha. "Call the police."

"Why?" said Natasha. "What is it?"

There was movement behind Natasha. Bernard appeared at the bottom of the stairs.

"What's going on, Nat?" he asked. "What's wrong?"

Natasha turned to him. "It's Simone apparently, something's happened." She turned back to Frankie and Adam. "You found her? Where is she now?"

"She's dead," said Adam. He had hold of Frankie's arm, his fingertips sharp through her thin jacket. "We found her on the beach."

"Dead?" said Natasha. "Don't be stupid. She was sick, she rang in."

"Did she?" said Frankie. "She rang you?"

Natasha blinked at her. "She rang here this morning. First thing. She spoke to Bernard." She turned to her husband. "Didn't she?"

He nodded. "They're right, love," he told his wife. "We should call the authorities."

Frankie looked into Natasha's face.

"Call the police," she said. "Now!"

"I need to tell Ed. He'll know what to do."

Ed was Natasha's boss, the person in charge of the full-time National Trust staff on the island.

Frankie shook her head. "There isn't time."

Bernard was behind Natasha, his hands on her shoulders. He looked at Adam. "It's dark. You're sure?"

Frankie felt heat surge through her body. "We're not imagining things."

He nodded. "No. Sorry. I'll make the call." He turned away. Frankie stared after him, wondering whether she should follow him inside, or go back to the beach.

Natasha reached out to a set of coat hooks behind the door. She grabbed a coat and slung it over her shoulders. "Show me. I need to see."

Frankie stared at her. "You don't."

Natasha glared at her. "Show me, Frankie."

Frankie exchanged a look with Adam. He shrugged. "OK," she said.

She turned away from the house and ran back towards the beach. She could hear two sets of footsteps behind her, Adam and Natasha.

They were at the beach in moments, much quicker than last time. She waved her arm in the direction of Simone's body. She didn't want to look at her again.

"Down there," she panted.

Natasha ran onto the beach. Frankie followed, slowly, her footsteps uneven.

"Is she still there?" she called, still holding out a glimmer of hope that she might have been wrong. That Simone might have stood up and walked away. Or that she might not have been there at all.

"She is," Natasha called. "It's Simone. Oh my God." The last word came out as a wail.

Adam was behind Frankie. "What's she doing?" he hissed.

"I don't know," she whispered. "We need to call the police."

She called out to Natasha. "Come away! Don't disturb her." It might be a crime scene, she realised with a jolt.

"Bernard's already doing it," Adam told her. "He's on the phone."

Natasha was walking back from the beach, her body a shadow against the night sky. She stumbled towards Frankie and grabbed her arm. "You're right," she breathed. "It's Simone, she's dead."

CHAPTER FOUR

A note was sitting on Lesley's desk when she arrived in the office: *Report to Detective Superintendent Carpenter's office asap*.

There was no signature, no indication of when it had been left. She left it sitting on the desk and went out into the team room. DS Dennis Frampton was alone at his desk, yawning and stretching his arms above his head. When he saw her, he jolted to attention.

"Have you seen anyone come into my office this morning and leave me a note?"

Dennis wiped his glasses and placed them back on his nose. "No, boss."

"Have you been here long?"

"I got here about ten minutes before you."

The door opened and DC Johnny Chiles entered.

"Morning, Johnny," Lesley said. "You've just arrived?"

He shrugged. "Er, yes boss. Am I late?"

It was eight thirty; he was early. "It's OK, Johnny," Lesley replied.

It didn't matter who'd left the note, or even when. She just needed to get to Carpenter's office. She didn't like the idea of him leaving her notes. Not that it was likely to have been him. When you got to the heady heights of Detective Superintendent, you had other people to do that kind of thing for you.

She hurried up the stairs, straightening her skirt, and knocked on his door.

"Come in," he called.

She entered and closed the door behind her. Carpenter had a large office at the front of the building, above her own but twice the size. Next to her was a desk, chairs placed on either side of it. In the far corner was a tight arrangement of easy chairs. Carpenter was in one of those chairs, reading a newspaper.

Lesley looked at him. "You wanted to see me, Sir."

He laid the newspaper down on the coffee table in front of him: the *Bournemouth Echo*. "Pays to keep on top of what's going on," he told her. "Not just the crime reporting."

She nodded. As a DCI, she didn't have to worry about that kind of thing, thank God. If she ever wanted promotion, she'd have to put up with less detecting and more politicking. Lesley wasn't sure she'd be very good at politicking.

"I can imagine, Sir," she replied.

He indicated for her to take one of the easy chairs. She picked the one next to him and sat tidily. She'd rather sit at his desk, but if he wanted to try to put her at her ease, she wouldn't argue.

He leaned back. "We've got a death on Brownsea Island."

"Brownsea Island?"

He steepled his hands in front of him. "It's delicate."

"In what way?" she asked, wondering who the victim might be. A member of the force? A local bigwig? "Who's the deceased?"

"Member of National Trust staff, name of Simone Browning," he told her.

"I haven't heard of her," Lesley replied.

"You wouldn't have. She was a specialist in squirrels, apparently."

Lesley stopped herself from laughing. "Squirrels? Do people even have jobs being specialists in squirrels?"

He cocked his head. "You don't know that Brownsea Island is known for its population of red squirrels?"

Lesley looked back at him, struggling to keep a straight face. "I didn't, Sir."

"You do now."

"So why is it delicate?" she asked. "Are we looking at a murder?"

"We don't know that yet. A call was made to 999 late last night. Uniform went over in a boat along with a couple of paramedics, but they were too late for this poor woman. She'd washed up on one of the beaches."

"And she worked there?"

"She did." He leaned forward. "Like much of the area, Brownsea is owned by the National Trust. Although John Lewis does have a slice of it."

"John Lewis?"

"The castle. You'll see."

Lesley nodded. She didn't understand what involvement a retailer would have with a castle on a National Trust island, but she'd find out soon enough. And there were more pressing questions than this one. "Have we closed the island off to visitors, Sir?" she asked.

"We have. No boats have run since yesterday afternoon. The John Lewis people aren't happy about it, they were due to have a delegation arrive today."

"I'm sure they'll understand."

He eyed her. "It'll be your job to smooth the waters."

She opened her mouth to object. Surely her job was to investigate Simone Browning's death. But if that involved a bit of PR, then she'd have to put up with it.

"Sir."

"Apparently she was a member of the island's conservation team. Lived there, with a bunch of other tree huggers. We need to handle this carefully, the National Trust are a major player in this county."

Lesley nodded. She rose from her chair. "I'll get straight over there. Take a team with me."

"We don't want to go in there mob-handed. Just take DS Frampton."

Lesley considered. There would be a handful of people to interview, this conservation team Carpenter had mentioned. If the woman had drowned herself, there wouldn't even be a crime to investigate. "No problem," she replied, turning for the door.

"Report back to me. And keep them sweet, will you?"

"Of course, Sir."

Lesley returned to the office to find Dennis standing over Johnny's desk. DC Mike Legg was with them. All three men were looking at Johnny's screen, a news report: *Body found on Brownsea Island.*

"So it's public," she said.

The three men looked up.

"Is this what Carpenter wanted you for?" asked Dennis.

"It was," she replied. "You and I need to go over to the island and find out if it's suspicious."

Dennis moved away from the back of Johnny's chair and walked to his own desk, still limping ever so slightly. His wound from when he'd taken Harry Nevin's killer had almost healed, but not as much as he liked to make out. Would he cope with taking a ferry across to the island?

Lesley knew better than to suggest to Dennis's face that he might not be up to the job. She would make sure he didn't have to do much yomping around once they got there. The tourists did the trip every day, and most of them were past their best from what Lesley had seen.

"Right," she said. "So how do we get over there?"

Mike looked up. "The National Trust run boats. Private ones, as well as the tourist ones."

"Good," said Lesley. "See if they'll get us over there on one, will you?"

"Boss." Mike picked up his phone.

Dennis looked at Lesley. "And I think you should take Johnny instead of me."

Lesley raised an eyebrow. Was he admitting that this was too much for him? "The Super mentioned you by name."

Dennis shook his head. "Look at me," he said. "I'm in no fit state to be getting boats and tramping across the island. Take Johnny, it'll be good experience for him."

Lesley looked between Johnny and Mike. "Just Johnny?"

"I'll need Mike here to help me collate evidence," Dennis said, just as the fifth member of the team entered: PC Tina Abbott.

Tina looked between the men, her face reddening. "Am I late? Was there a briefing?"

Lesley smiled at her. "It's fine, Tina. Carpenter's got us on the Brownsea Island case. I imagine you've heard all about it already."

Tina placed her uniform jacket on the back of her chair. Her face was grave. "Nasty business, boss. Poor woman."

"I'm heading over there, with Johnny. We'll find out if it's suspicious, and if it is, we'll allocate resources."

"Anything I can do while you're gone?"

"Don't worry, Constable," said Dennis. "I'll keep you busy."

Tina looked from Lesley to Dennis and back again. "Of course."

"That's settled then," said Lesley. "Johnny, you drive."

It would be a quick jaunt over to Brownsea Island, discover they had a suicide on their hands, and then back to report to Carpenter. It didn't really matter who she took.

CHAPTER FIVE

"So," said Lesley as she and Johnny approached Poole Quay. "Brownsea Island, have you been there much?"

Johnny poked his tongue between his teeth, concentrating on squeezing into the multi-storey car park.

"Never, boss," he replied.

"Never?" she said. "I thought you'd lived down here all your life?"

He turned a tight corner, eyeing a space ahead of them. "I'm inland, near Dorchester. I don't go to the sea that much."

She laughed. For her, Midlands born and bred, the sea was the main attraction of being in Dorset. She liked to drag Elsa out for evening walks along the beach.

"Never?" she said. "Not even when you were a kid?"

"When I was a kid, yeah. Mum and Dad used to bring me down to Bournemouth beach all the time. I wasn't that keen, though."

"How can you not be keen on the beach when you're a kid?"

He eased the car into the space and turned off the ignition.

He turned to her. "You won't tell the sarge this, will you?"

She smiled at him. "Depends what it is."

He gave her a serious look.

"No," she said. "I won't tell him." She wondered what Johnny's big secret was.

"I get seasick," he replied. "I can't stand being out on the water."

"Seasick?"

He nodded. "I'm not much of a Dorset dumpling, am I?"

"Dorset dumpling?"

A smile played at the corners of his lips. "Local phrase, Dorset born and bred. I don't fit though, not if I don't like the sea. Poole Harbour dominates this county."

She shrugged. "I guess there are plenty of places inland." She eyed him. "Anyway, are you going to be alright on this boat?"

He grimaced. "I'll hold my breath."

She closed the door to the car and followed Johnny out of the car park. Moments later, they were standing on the quay next to a hexagonal kiosk painted a bright orange. *Brownsea Island Tours.* Crowds of people flocked around it, queuing haphazardly to buy their tickets.

Lesley checked her watch. It was two hours since Carpenter had called her into his office. She didn't like this taking so long.

The crowd was getting agitated. The man in the kiosk, an old guy with weatherworn skin, was trying to explain that he wasn't sailing today. Lesley pushed through and approached him.

"DCI Clarke, Dorset Police," she muttered. "Everything alright here?"

He looked at her. "National Trust have closed the island. Your lot told them to, apparently."

Good. She didn't want hordes of grockles tramping all over a crime scene. "Makes sense."

"You going to compensate me?"

Lesley pointed at her chest in a *who, me?* gesture. "Dorset Police?"

He nodded, his lips tight.

She laughed. "Sorry, mate. If the island needs to be closed off, it needs to be closed off. I suggest you take it up with the National Trust." It wasn't as if they were short of cash, what with the money they took from all the buildings, beaches and car parks they owned.

He gave her a look that told her he'd have little joy in that endeavour. "The quicker you get your job done, the sooner I can get back to work. I'm losing thousands every day."

A woman's dead, Lesley stopped herself from saying. After all, it was August, and this man ran a business ferrying holidaymakers back and forth across Poole Harbour. She could understand his disgruntlement.

"I'm sure someone will let you know as soon as you can start sailing again," she told him.

She turned away and struggled through the crowd. Johnny was a few metres away, talking to a slim man with thinning hair who wore a National Trust t-shirt. The man held out a hand as Lesley approached. She took it.

"You must be DCI Clarke," he said. "I'm Ed Rogers, island manager. Call me Ed."

"You're going to be able to get us over there?" she asked. "Despite the ferry not running?"

He looked past her at the crowds around the kiosk. "Poor Sam," he said. "His job won't be easy today. I'll send a couple of volunteers over to give him a hand, it's not like they've got anything else to do."

She nodded: no compensation, but at least he was aware of the ferry owner's problems.

"Come with me," Ed said. "We've got our boat here."

Johnny was staring past the island manager towards a small boat with no more than ten seats. Lesley gave him a squeeze on the arm. "Don't worry, it's not far."

He swallowed and nodded, his expression grim.

They approached the boat, which had a tiny cabin on the front and rolled in the sway of the water.

"Christ," muttered Johnny. He looked over at the out-of-service tourist boat with its fully enclosed lower deck, and at least a hundred seats up top.

"It'll be fine," Lesley told him. The day was bright, the harbour sparkling in the sunshine and the water calm. "Look, perfect weather for a sail."

Ed was unhooking ropes from a mooring next to the boat. "You're not happy on the water?"

Johnny shook his head. "I'll be fine, don't worry."

Lesley smiled. Johnny was going to struggle to keep this from Dennis.

She took Ed's proffered hand and let him guide her into the boat, taking a seat as close to the centre as she could. Johnny sat in front of her, his gaze intent on the horizon. She looked behind them at the large boat, empty of tourists. Hopefully, they'd let Sam get back to business soon.

Ed untied more ropes and clambered down into the boat, making it sway. He went to the open cabin at the front and started the engine. Lesley wanted to start asking questions, but as soon as the engine came to life, its noise covered her voice. She slumped into her seat as the boat headed out into the harbour. Johnny gripped his seat. His mouth was a straight line, his eyes closed. She wanted to lean over and reassure him, give him a friendly tap on the shoulder, but she worried that might make him worse.

Just don't chuck up on me, she thought.

Fifteen minutes later, they were approaching the island. The boat had taken a looping route towards the mouth of the harbour and then made a right turn in towards the castle, which dominated this side of the island. They passed a wide lagoon, the air above filled with birds. The noise was like nothing she'd ever heard.

Lesley wished she'd taken some time to gen up on this place, to discover what that castle was and who she might expect to find here. Were there many people living on this island, or did most of the workers and volunteers commute across the harbour every day?

As they neared the quay, she saw two figures waiting. Gail, the crime scene manager, and her colleague Gavin, the ridiculously tall CSI. Gail heard the boat and turned, raising an arm to shield her eyes from the sun. She gave a wave which Lesley returned. It was good to see a familiar face. Gail wouldn't be fighting nausea, she'd have invest-igated the lie of the land and would be able to fill Lesley in.

The boat pulled in next to the quay and Ed climbed out. A man and a woman in National Trust t-shirts helped him secure the boat. The woman held out a hand and Lesley let her help her up the steep steps. Lesley turned to see Johnny climbing up behind her, his face grey, his movements slow.

She grabbed his hand, which was clammy. "Are you going to be alright?" she muttered.

He nodded, then clenched his eyes shut, regretting moving his head.

Lesley took a deep breath as she spotted a bench over to one side. The quay was quiet, a low building behind it and the castle beyond that. Birds swooped and dived above their heads, and all around was the smell of the sea. The tarmac was spattered with bird droppings.

"Sit down there," she told Johnny. "Put your head between your legs, you'll be right as rain in five minutes."

She turned to Ed. "OK," she said. "Show me where they found her."

CHAPTER SIX

Gail hurried to keep up with Lesley and Johnny as they walked behind Ed through the buildings beyond the quay. She was lugging a flight case and had a large black holdall slung over her shoulder. She wore sturdy walking boots. Lesley had on her brown leather ankle boots, not as practical as she'd have liked but better than the heels she'd been in the habit of wearing back in Birmingham.

"Have you been to the crime scene yet?" Lesley asked.

"Not yet," the CSM replied. "We only just got here. They brought us in on their cargo boat."

She pointed past Lesley out into the harbour where a flat-bottomed boat was moored.

Lesley eyed Johnny. "Think yourself lucky you didn't come in on that."

He shook his head, silent. The colour was coming back to his cheeks but he hadn't spoken since they'd left Poole Quay. She hoped he was going to be more use to her once he recovered.

"D'you know the island well?" Lesley asked Gail.

"I've been out here about half a dozen times. Day trips, looking for squirrels, watching the birds. My ex was into that sort of thing."

"Are there people who live here?"

"I think there's about forty of them."

Ed, who was walking ahead of them, turned. "There are forty-two people living on the island currently," he said. "Thirty-three of those are National Trust employees, the others work for John Lewis."

"John Lewis," Lesley asked. "I don't understand the connection?"

Ed pointed towards the castle they'd passed as they left the boat. "That's leased by John Lewis, they use it as a hotel for their employees, or rather their partners. The nine people who live there work in the hotel."

"And do you work closely with them?" Lesley asked.

He shook his head. "They tend to keep themselves to themselves. We see their people coming in and out on their own boat, but they don't mix with the tourists, and they don't have much to do with our team."

Lesley nodded. "We'll need to talk to them as well as your people."

"Fair enough," he said. "You'll need to speak to the hotel manager. Yolanda Harte."

They were walking past tall gates that led to the back of the castle, heading towards a broad grassy area with a church beyond.

"Does that church serve the people who live here?" Lesley asked.

"It runs one service a week," he said. "People come over from the mainland especially. We get a good crowd in, generally not National Trust staff. Older people from Bournemouth and the surrounding areas."

Lesley looked at the church. It was imposing, much bigger than you'd expect on a small island like Brownsea. She wondered how it had come to be built. Surely the place hadn't had much of a population at any time in its history?

They took a left turn and walked across the grass. Lesley heard a shriek and stopped walking. Johnny stumbled into her and groaned.

"Sorry, Johnny," she said. "What was that?"

Ed smiled at her. "Our resident peacock. Noisy bugger."

Lesley breathed a sigh of relief. She'd never heard a noise like it. She scanned the grassy area looking for the bird, but couldn't see it. The sound had come from the church. She wondered if there was just one of them, or a whole flock.

"This way." Ed strode past a set of dilapidated buildings onto a narrow lane that seemed to lead back towards the coast.

"This is the old farm," Gail said. "When the old woman who used to own this place lived here, it was a working farm. Now they use it as a museum."

Lesley nodded. "You've got people who work here?" Lesley asked Ed.

"Not full time staff. Volunteers. Adam Stanley's the volunteer manager, you'll meet him. He's one of the couple who found the body."

"Where are all your staff?" Lesley asked. The island had been eerily quiet so far.

"I told them to go home, to wait until they were summoned by police. I trust that was the right thing to do?"

"It was," she replied. *Forty-two people*, she thought. They would need more bodies over here, uniformed constables to knock on doors and ask questions.

"Wait a moment," Lesley said to Ed.

She turned to Johnny. "How are you feeling?" she asked him.

"I'll do," he replied. "You need me to start the interviews?"

Lesley smiled, relieved he was back to being a copper instead of an invalid. "Start talking to some of the people who live here. Get some names, find out who knew the dead woman."

She looked to Ed. "Who were the couple that found her?"

"Adam Stanley and Frankie Quinn," he replied. "She's a bird specialist. They live in one of the houses up past the church, on the Poole side of the island. Do you want me to show you?" he asked Johnny.

Johnny looked at Lesley.

"No," she said. "I need to see the crime scene first. Johnny, do you think you can find your way?"

"Is there a path, mate?" Johnny asked Ed.

"Go up to the church, turn left and keep walking past the lagoon and the reed beds. You can't miss it. It's a heavy building on the right-hand side split into two houses. Frankie lives in one, Simone in the other."

Lesley knew that name. "Simone Browning, the victim?"

Ed nodded.

"Does anybody else live there with her?"

Ed shook his head. "She lived alone. Frankie lives with Adam."

"And they'll be at home right now?"

"I asked everybody to stay home."

Lesley turned to Johnny. "Let me know how you get on."

"Will do, boss." He hurried away.

Gail was ahead of them. Lesley and Ed increased their pace and caught her up. "How far are we from this beach?" Lesley asked.

"A couple of minutes tops," Ed said. "Not far now."

"Good." Lesley didn't much relish undertaking this journey every time she had to visit the crime scene. All the way across the harbour, and then the walk to the beach.

"Is the beach accessible for a boat?" she asked.

"It had better be," Gail said. "We'll need to bring kit in. And search for evidence out in the shallows."

Ed frowned. "Just don't let the public know," he said. "I don't want people thinking they can just moor up on these beaches."

"Don't worry," Lesley told him. "I think you'll find we're a special case."

CHAPTER SEVEN

Dennis circled the desks for the fourth time. Mike kept glancing up at him, his body language uneasy. Tina stared at her screen, pretending she hadn't noticed his agitation.

He checked his phone again. He didn't like this, the boss and Johnny off to the crime scene, the rest of them back in the office not knowing what was going on. Dennis was used to going out to crime scenes with Johnny, or at least with the DCI.

He called her again. No answer, again.

He slammed his phone onto his desk. "Do you know what the signal is like over on Brownsea Island?" he asked no one in particular.

Mike looked up. "I can't see why they wouldn't have any. There's plenty of people over there."

Dennis raised an eyebrow. "You've been doing some research?"

"I have, Sarge."

Mike gave him a wary look, as if he was weighing up whether he should provide Dennis with more information. It might calm the sergeant down, but it might have the opposite effect.

"Go on," Dennis snapped. He sank into his chair. "Tell me what you've got, it'll take my mind off it."

Mike cleared his throat and looked at his screen.

"So," he said, "Most of the people living over there work for the National Trust, conservation people, volunteer and visitor management, maintenance workers, that kind of thing."

"How many of them?" Dennis asked.

"Well, there's forty-two in total… I'm not sure how many of those are National Trust. Then there'll be people who work there and commute across the harbour."

"How many? A hundred?"

Mike shrugged. "No idea. There are also people from John Lewis."

"John Lewis?"

Mike nodded. "They're in the hotel, the castle. You know it?"

Dennis nodded. "I always thought it was National Trust, like the rest."

"It's leased by John Lewis, only their staff can stay there."

"Nice. Why don't the police do things like that?"

Mike laughed nervously. *Calm down*, Dennis told himself.

It was a few years since he'd been to Brownsea Island, him and Pam going for a picnic on a sunny Saturday afternoon. But he remembered the castle appearing on the shoreline as they approached the island in the boat. Pam had been disappointed that it was closed to visitors; she'd been expecting a tour of a stately home.

Dennis slumped into his chair. "But our victim, she was National Trust. Yes?"

"Yes, boss," said Mike.

"I've got more information," said Tina. "I've spoken to the National Trust."

Dennis pushed his chair over towards her. "Well done. What have you got?"

"Names. Ed Rogers, he's the manager for the National Trust over there. He supervises the various teams that manage the island. And then there's a woman called Yolanda Harte. She's in charge at the hotel, the castle, she works for John Lewis. The person I spoke to at the National Trust only had her name from the John Lewis lot, but they can send us a list of all the National Trust people over there."

"Good," Dennis said. "Get on to John Lewis as well. I want the names of the people working in that hotel."

"What about visitors?" Mike suggested "No reason why one of them couldn't have seen what happened."

"Or have been involved." Dennis felt a shiver run down his spine. "Any more names?" he asked Tina.

Tina nodded. "Natasha Williams, she's a team leader for the Conservation team. The woman they found dead, Simone, she works for Natasha."

"Right," said Dennis, "So we need to talk to Natasha Williams, find out what we can about our victim."

"I'll let Johnny know," said Tina.

"It's all right," replied Dennis. "I'll call the boss."

He grabbed his phone from his desk and was about to dial the DCI yet again when it rang. He felt relief wash through him. At last they were being brought into the investigation.

"Looks like she's got there before me," he said.

CHAPTER EIGHT

Simone Browning's body was still on the beach where it had been found. The tide had gone out and her body lay on the rough sand, surrounded by driftwood.

Two uniformed officers were stringing tape across the edge of the beach. One of them looked out to sea, trying to work out how he might close off the scene in that direction.

Gail gripped her bag tightly and rushed ahead. She knelt on the ground next to the body.

"Poor woman," she muttered as Lesley approached.

Lesley stood over her, peering down at their victim. Simone Browning lay face upwards, her eyes staring at the sky. She had long blonde hair, frizzy and matted with sand, and she looked to be in her mid-thirties. She wore a National Trust fleece and a pair of worn jeans. No shoes.

Lesley wondered what had happened to this woman in her final moments. Had she done this to herself or had somebody done it to her?

"There's bloating," Gail said. "Her skin's puckered, but there's no gloving."

Gloving was the process of the skin peeling off the body after it had been submerged in water for a period of time.

"So she hasn't been there all that long?" Lesley asked.

Gail looked up at her. "We'll need the pathologist to confirm it, but I don't reckon so."

"When d'you think she washed up?"

"I'll have to check the tide charts," Gail replied. "I imagine on the last high tide before she was discovered."

"How often does the tide come in here?"

"Twice a day," Gail said. "Just like the rest of the harbour."

Lesley looked out to sea. The harbour on this side was quiet, the view of the dark Purbeck hills to the south. A few boats moved slowly in the water, closer to the mainland.

"We need to check for abandoned boats," she said. "She might have been pushed off one."

"Or pushed herself," Gail added.

Lesley nodded. "Is there anywhere on the island she might have gone into the water?"

"Plenty of spots. There are other beaches and the quay. More than that, I imagine."

Lesley looked down at Simone. What would it take for a person to wade into the sea and allow themselves to be overcome by the water?

She needed to know what was going on in this woman's life, if she'd been suicidal, if she'd fallen out with any of her colleagues. And then there were the hundreds of visitors coming here every day. She needed names.

She looked up to see Ed standing at the top of the beach, watching them. He held his hands by his sides, clenching and unclenching his fists. The man clearly didn't want to come any closer. Lesley trudged back up the beach, glad she'd worn sensible shoes, and stood next to him.

"What can you tell me about Simone's relationships with the other staff on the island?" she asked.

He shrugged. "Her line manager's Natasha. She's good, looks after her team. I'm not aware of any problems. But I'll check, if you—"

"My DC will speak to her. Anyone else? Who did she socialise with?"

Another shrug. "The members of her team, as far as I'm aware. I don't keep tabs on that kind of thing."

Lesley gazed towards Gail, who was examining the ground around Simone. This was a small community, only forty-two people. She found it hard to believe the man who managed it wouldn't make it his business to know that kind of thing.

"Have you got a key to Simone's house?" she asked.

"I can get one," Ed replied.

"Good. We'll need to search it, in case she left anything behind that might shed light on her death."

Ed nodded, his face grim.

"I'll send Brett over," said Gail. "Gav and I can join him when we're done here, if it looks like there's a lot to search through."

"Thanks," Lesley replied. She turned to Ed. "And I also need a list of all the visitors who came here in the last three days," she said.

"Three days?" he asked.

"Probably the last twenty-four hours," she said. "But we can't be too careful."

"We don't keep lists," he said. "I can identify any Trust members who were on the island, but non-members…" He shook his head.

"Give me what you can," she told him. "We can use credit card receipts if people paid for anything while they were here. Is there a café or a shop?"

"Both," he told her. "I'll speak to the relevant managers."

"Thank you." She looked back towards the body. This was a complex crime scene, despite its apparent simplicity. This particular stretch of beach was narrow and shallow. There was no sign of footsteps other than their own, and those of the two Uniforms. But Simone could have gone into the water anywhere. She could have gone in under her own volition, or somebody else's. There was also the possibility that she didn't go into the water from the island, but from somewhere else in Poole Harbour.

Lesley looked over towards the Isle of Purbeck. There were miles of shoreline over there, even more if you followed the coast round to Poole. They needed to narrow things down.

It was most likely that Simone had gone in from somewhere on the island. She lived there. She worked there. But Lesley wanted to check the woman's habits. And for any missing boats.

Gail's phone rang, the noise echoing across the space and sending a flock of small wading birds into the air. Lesley watched her answer it, expectant. Gail spoke and nodded a few times, and then shoved the phone into the pocket of her protective suit.

Gail stood up. "Good news. Whittaker is on his way."

Lesley raised an eyebrow. Henry Whittaker was the local pathologist. Not known for his reliability or speed, Lesley was surprised that he was already en route to such a remote crime scene.

"We're in luck," she said.

Gail gave a grim laugh. "Lucky for Simone she was found on a weeknight."

CHAPTER NINE

Lesley turned away from the beach. "I'll make sure he knows where to come," she told Gail. "Besides, I want to get a feel for the geography here."

She beckoned for Ed to come with her, and together they walked back towards the old farm buildings they'd passed on the way in.

"Tell me about your team," she said to him.

He nodded, his face stern. "I've got four team leaders reporting to me. Natasha runs the conservation team, Simone worked for her. And then there's the catering team, the volunteer manager, the maintenance team, and the shop."

"That's five teams," Lesley told him.

He closed his eyes. "Sorry," he said, running his hand through his hair. "I think I'm in shock."

Lesley eyed him. The man's reaction seemed genuine enough, but until she'd spoken to everybody on this island, she wasn't making any judgments.

They reached the expanse of grass in front of the church. There was no sign or sound of the peacock this time.

Lesley pulled out her phone. "I need to brief my DS," she said. "Can you go ahead and tell the pathologist where we are?"

"No problem," Ed replied. He trudged on towards the castle and the quay beyond, his footsteps heavy.

Dennis answered on the first ring. "Boss," he said. "What's happening?"

She looked up towards the church, admiring the stained-glass windows. "Got a body washed up on a beach on the southern side of Brownsea Island," she told him. "Gail's going to look into the tide patterns, but if one of you could get a start on that it would be helpful."

"No problem," he said.

"Can you put me on speakerphone?" she asked him.

"Ummm…"

Lesley chuckled. Dennis wasn't the most technical of sergeants.

"Hand the phone to Mike," she said. "He'll do it."

There was rustling at the other end of the line and then Dennis's voice came over. It was tinny and distant.

"We're in your office, boss," he said. "I'm with Mike and Tina."

"Good," she told him. "So what have you got? Have you done any research?"

"I've got the names of the staff you need to talk to," Tina said.

Lesley clutched her phone closer to her ear. "Ed Rogers, Natasha Williams."

"Oh," Tina replied, sounding deflated.

"It's all right, Tina," Lesley said. "I've got Ed with me, or did have until a moment ago. But anything you can get in the meantime is helpful. Get everything you can on the staff. Who works for who, who lives where on the island, and in particular, we need to know who was here during the last twenty-four hours."

"Can't you ask Ed that?" suggested Dennis.

"I'll be asking quite a few people that question," she replied. "But we need to know if there are any official records. Do they keep records of the boat when it goes out, who travels on it?"

"No problem, boss," said Dennis. "The National Trust office in Poole will be able to answer that question."

"Good," she said. "Whittaker is on his way, so hopefully we'll have a cause of death soon. And a time."

"Surely drowning?" Dennis replied.

"Let's not jump to conclusions," Lesley told him.

"You think it's suspicious?" he asked.

"I don't think anything just yet," Lesley said. "We'll base any conclusions on the facts. But in the meantime, we'll need more manpower. This is a big island and we've got forty-two people living here. Johnny and I can't cover them all on our own, at least not before they get the chance to share their stories with each other. I need more uniformed officers, and I need one of you."

Lesley considered the team's skills.

"Tina," she said, "you get on the next boat over to the island."

"Er, boss," Dennis said. "Surely Mike would be better placed…"

"Send Tina. You and Mike gather evidence back at the office, get background information. I'll keep you posted."

"No problem, boss," Dennis said. His voice sounded tight.

CHAPTER TEN

Frankie opened her door to find a skinny blonde man in his mid-thirties standing on the path outside. He wore a badly fitting blue suit and a look of queasiness.

"Hello?" she said. "Are you OK?"

The man looked pale and sweaty, like he might pass out at any minute.

He blinked at her and fumbled in his inside pocket. "Detective Constable Chiles," he said as he pulled out his ID.

She bristled. This man wasn't what she'd been expecting. "You're here to talk to me about Simone?"

He nodded. "Can I come in?"

"Of course."

She turned away from the door, leaving the constable to follow her, and walked through to the kitchen at the back of the house. Adam was already there, sitting at the kitchen table. He was on his laptop – reading the news, no doubt. He'd been obsessed with it since they'd found Simone, searching for any mention of what had happened.

The police officer nodded as he entered the kitchen.

Adam half-stood from his seat. "Hello," he said, looking wary. "You must be—?"

"DC Chiles," the officer replied.

Adam looked him up and down, clearly thinking the same thing as Frankie.

Frankie gestured towards the table. "Take a seat," she said. "I'll get you a coffee."

Adam stood up and put a hand on her arm. "It's OK love, I'll do it."

She gave him a grateful smile and sat down.

The constable sat opposite her. He cleared his throat and swallowed.

Just don't throw up on my kitchen table. She wondered if he'd come straight from the quay.

After a moment's uncomfortable silence, the constable brought a notepad out of the same pocket from which he'd extracted his ID earlier.

"I need to ask what happened last night," he said. "When you found her."

"Simone," she replied.

He nodded. "Sorry, yes. Do you work with her?"

"I do," she told him. "Or I did." She felt her stomach grow heavy.

At the sink, Adam was rattling around, as if he was trying to drown out the sound of their voices. But he'd been there too, he was a witness. They might as well do this together.

The constable looked at Adam as he put a cup of coffee in front of him.

"I'm told you both found the body," he said.

"It was Frankie who spotted her first," Adam replied. "Then I…" He retreated to the sink, his voice thin.

"I'll need to speak to the two of you separately." The constable looked at Frankie. "Do you mind if we go into another room?"

She exchanged glances with Adam.

"It's OK," Adam said. "You two stay in here, I'll go upstairs." He grabbed his laptop from the table and left the room.

Frankie heard his footsteps on the stairs above their head. Hurried, anxious. She imagined he'd keep a door open to listen in.

She wrapped her hands around her mug of coffee, which was going cold. "Go on, then," she said to the officer. "Ask your questions."

"I'm sorry to have to do this," he told her. "I know it must be traumatic for you."

She shook her head. "For all of us," she said. "But I know why you're here."

He raised an eyebrow.

"You don't believe me," she said. "You think that by saying I found her body, that'll cover up any suspicion that I might have done it."

The officer frowned at her. "That's not what I was thinking at all. I just wanted to get your account of what you saw."

"Oh." She looked down at her mug.

Stop being so nervous. It wasn't her fault she'd been the person to come across Simone. It wasn't her fault they'd fallen out. But the detective didn't know that.

She looked into his eyes, forcing herself to hold his gaze.

"It was after the team meeting," she said. "Simone hadn't turned up, she'd been off sick for the day, at least that's what Bernard told us."

"Bernard is…?" he asked.

"Sorry, he's Natasha's husband. Natasha is my line manager, she supervises the conservation team. Bernard, he lives with her."

"And does he work here as well?"

"No," she said. "He's a freelance journalist. Works from home, mainly."

"OK. So you were at Natasha's house, and then you left at what time?"

She thought back. "About ten, just before. Adam was outside when I left, he'd been waiting for me. We go down to the beach sometimes at night." She smiled. "It's our place."

"And that's where you found Simone," the officer suggested.

She swallowed. "It was getting dark," she said. "Cloudy. We were almost on top of her when I saw her."

"And it was you who saw her first?"

"Yes. Adam was behind me. I told him to come and see, and then we went back to Natasha's house."

"So you left Simone's body where you'd found it, and you went back to Natasha's?"

"Yes," she said.

"Did you touch the body at all? Did you move it?"

She stared at him, blinking. "No. No."

She shivered. The thought of touching Simone, the way she'd been, filled her with horror.

"She was on the edge of the water, the waves were washing over her. But still, I couldn't bring myself to…"

"It's OK." The constable put a hand on the table, a few centimetres from her own. She stared at it, resisting the urge to pull back. "It's good that you didn't touch the body," he continued. "It preserves any evidence there might be on it."

"Evidence," she repeated, looking down into her mug.

"Did you see anyone else, on your way to the beach?"

"No one. People are all in their houses by that time of night. We rise early, like the wildlife."

He nodded. "So you went back to Natasha's house. And then what happened?"

"We knocked on the door. It took a few minutes to get Natasha's attention, I think she was going to bed. We told her what we'd seen and she insisted on going down to the beach."

He looked surprised. "Any idea why?"

She shook her head. "Maybe she didn't believe us, maybe she wanted to see for herself. We wanted to call the police or the coastguard, but Natasha wanted to see."

Another frown. "So the three of you went down to the beach?"

"Yes. And then Natasha saw, and we hurried back to her house while her husband called the police."

"Was anybody else with you? Natasha's husband?"

"No, he stayed at the house."

"That's fine," the officer said. "I know this is difficult for you to talk about."

"I'm OK," she told him.

She hated the way she'd collapsed into herself since finding Simone's body. Frankie prided herself on being strong. Since leaving her first marriage, she'd had to fend for herself, to forge her own way in the world. Even now she had Adam, she wasn't relinquishing her independence for a second.

But now… here she was, a gibbering wreck.

"How did she die?" she asked him.

"We don't know yet. The pathologist should be on his way and then we'll know."

"You think she killed herself, or…?"

"Like I say," he replied, shifting his fingers on the table. "We don't know yet." He took a breath. "So after you called the police, what happened then?"

"They told us to wait."

"In the house?"

"No," she said. "They told us to go somewhere we'd be able to stop people going down there."

"So where did you go?"

His eyes searched her face. She could tell he was hoping they hadn't gone straight back to the beach. Frankie had watched enough police dramas to know that disturbing a crime scene was not a good idea.

"We went to the farm," she said. "The abandoned farm buildings at the top of the path that leads to the beach. Anybody going down there would have to go past us."

"And did anybody try to pass?" he asked.

"No," she said. "The first people to arrive were the Coast Guard."

"Good."

He stood up from his chair. "So can you tell me who else is in your team?"

"There's Natasha and then there's Anya."

"What does Anya do?"

"She works on habitats, she sometimes helps out with the volunteers as well."

"It was just the three of you at the meeting last night?" She nodded.

"Where can I find Anya?"

"She lives in one of the houses over by the quay," Frankie told him. "Simone lives next door to us. Or she did." She felt her stomach lurch.

He went to the door, glancing upwards. Adam's turn next. "Does anyone else live here, apart from you and Adam?"

"My son, Cameron. He's not here right now, though. He's in London, with his dad." She didn't like Cameron staying with Howard, it made her jumpy. She sniffed and looked at the officer. "Do you need anything else from me?"

He shook his head. "I'll go and talk to your partner now, if that's OK?"

She rubbed her eyes. "Of course. I'll call him down."

"Thank you."

CHAPTER ELEVEN

Lesley turned to see a commotion behind her. Dr Whittaker was scrambling down the steps towards the beach, looking out of place in a pale grey suit that hung off him. The man had lost weight. She wondered if he was ill, or maybe trying to get healthy. Two pathology assistants followed him, both looking stern and business-like.

Lesley stood up. Gail was in the process of placing squares on the beach, recording the areas that had been examined for forensic evidence.

"Dr Whittaker," Lesley said. "Thanks for coming out."

He grunted. "The chaps from the National Trust brought me. You do like dragging me out to these far flung places don't you, Detective Chief Inspector?"

She gave him a grim smile. "Not my fault where people die."

He grunted again and pushed past her. "So, let's take a look." He crouched over the body. He sniffed and tilted his head to get a better look.

"What do you think the cause of death is?" asked Lesley.

He glanced up at her. "Give me a moment, won't you?"

She tapped her foot and folded her arms. Whittaker was never easy to deal with, but today he was even grumpier than usual. She wondered if the weight loss had something to do with it. A diet would make him irritable, and so would an illness.

"Hmm," he said, leaning back.

He reached out a hand and one of his assistants pulled him up to a standing position.

"So, there are traces of foam around her mouth," he said. "That would indicate drowning."

Lesley nodded. She'd spotted that herself.

"When was she found?" he asked her. "Who was here?"

"Last night," she said. "By two National Trust employees. Around ten pm."

Another grunt. "Did they think to make a record of what state the body was in at the time?"

Lesley hadn't had a chance to ask that question herself. She beckoned Ed over. He was standing at the back of the beach, surveying proceedings.

He approached very deliberately, careful not to look in the direction of the body.

"This is Ed Rogers," she said. "He's the manager for the National Trust on this island."

Whittaker nodded at the man. "Were you here when she was found?"

"I didn't come down onto the beach," Ed replied. "The paramedics told me not to disturb the scene."

"Very sensible of them. So there were paramedics?"

Ed nodded. "They came in with the coastguard, first people who could get here."

"And did they say anything about the state of the body at the time?"

A shrug. "She was stiff, from what I remember them saying. They didn't talk to me, they came in, barked a few things at each other, and then hurried away. They weren't interested once they knew she was dead."

Lesley frowned. Normally paramedics had the best bedside manner of all health professionals. They were used to dealing with members of the public right at the beginning of their journey through the health system. But being called out to Brownsea Island at almost midnight wouldn't make anybody particularly sympathetic.

"But they said she was stiff?" she asked.

Ed nodded.

"She still is," said Whittaker. "As a general rule of thumb, decomposition takes twice as long when a body is submerged in water. When was the last high tide?"

Lesley turned to Ed.

"Yesterday evening. Early, about seven."

Whittaker nodded. "She could have been washed up then, or possibly in a previous tide. Do people come down here a lot?"

"They don't," said Ed. "Sometimes you get visitors down here, but none of my team are working on this part of the island right now."

"We need to find out if any tourists spotted anything," said Lesley. "Are you working on that list?" she asked Ed.

"I've got someone in the admin office collating it right now."

"Thanks."

"So," Whittaker said, balling his fists into the small of his back and stretching. The skin on his face was loose. However he'd lost the weight, it had come off fast.

"She definitely drowned," he said. "The foaming around her mouth. I'll be able to confirm when I look at her lungs during the post-mortem. And I estimate, based on the fact that rigor is still visible, that she died around twenty to thirty hours ago."

That was too wide a window. "She wasn't seen yesterday," Lesley said. "She called in sick on Tuesday morning, yes?"

Ed nodded. "Her line manager is Natasha, she'll be able to tell you more."

"My DC's already talking to her."

"Right." Whittaker grabbed Lesley's arm, making her flinch. He gave Ed a *leave us* look as he pulled Lesley down towards the body. He pointed to the woman's neck.

Lesley bent to get a better view. There was bruising on the side of her neck. Circles, purple with yellow edges.

"Fingerprints," she muttered.

Whittaker nodded. "Cause of death is drowning, as far as I can tell right now. But someone did that to her."

She looked at him. Ed had moved away and was on his phone.

"It's a murder case," she breathed.

"That's how it looks, yes," said Whittaker.

Lesley looked back towards Ed, who'd pocketed his phone and was approaching. She stood up.

Whittaker let go of her arm. "We'll move her now. If you can all stand aside."

He nodded towards his two assistants. They opened a large black holdall and brought out a body bag.

"Hang on a minute," Lesley said. She waved Gail over. "Are you ready for them to move the body yet?"

"Fine by me," Gail said. "Keep her out here any longer, what with the sand and the sea, and any evidence on the body could be contaminated."

"OK," said Lesley. She nodded at Whittaker's two assistants.

He gave her a harsh look, his small blue eyes flashing in the low sun. "Glad to see I've got your permission, Detective Chief Inspector."

She ignored the barb. "Let me know when you're doing the post-mortem, won't you?"

CHAPTER TWELVE

Natasha Williams lived in a low cottage beyond the crime scene, looking through trees towards the harbour and the Isle of Purbeck beyond. Johnny stamped his feet and hunched his shoulders as he waited for the door to be opened. He didn't like being this close to the cliffs and he certainly wasn't looking forward to the return trip to the mainland. He pushed the thought of it out of his mind and focused on the questions he was going to ask this woman.

The door opened, and a thin, curly-haired woman wearing a National Trust fleece stood looking at him. She blinked into the brightness of the day.

"You must be the police," she said.

He gave her a grim smile. "Sorry to bother you, but your colleague, Frankie Quinn, she told me..."

Natasha waved her hand in dismissal. "I know what she told you. It was me who called the coastguard. Well, it was Bernard, my husband, but I told him to. I wanted to see the body."

Johnny nodded. "Can I come in please?"

"No problem."

The woman held the door wider and stood back to let him pass. She gestured towards a door to the left, and Johnny shuffled through into a cosy kitchen. A pot of tea sat on the table and he could smell meat roasting. He inhaled, glad that the nausea had passed.

"Sit down," she said. "Do you want a coffee?"

"Cup of tea, please, if you don't mind."

Tea would do him good, get some liquid into his system. Even better if she had biscuits. His eyes roamed the kitchen, looking for a tin. Sure enough there was one sitting next to the teapot on the table. He salivated in anticipation, hoping she'd offer him one.

He thought of the times when he was a kid and had been travel sick on long journeys. His mum had fed him Rich Tea biscuits, something plain to settle his stomach, she'd told him. At the very least they'd distracted him, kept his mouth busy sending things down instead of bringing things up. It was illogical, but it seemed to work.

He took a seat at the table, facing the window and the sink in front of it. Natasha filled the kettle and turned to him while it was boiling.

"What's your name?" she asked him.

"Sorry," he said. "DC Chiles." He ferreted in his pocket and pulled out his badge, but she waved it away. "I'm here with the senior investigating officer, DCI Clarke."

The woman raised an eyebrow. "So there's been a crime?"

He felt himself blush. "We don't know yet. Hopefully you can help us get a better understanding."

Natasha turned away towards the kettle. It clicked and she picked it up. She frowned, peering around the room until her gaze landed on the teapot in the middle of the table. She put the kettle down and grabbed the teapot, taking it to the sink where she emptied it and then refilled it again. She brought the teapot to the table with two mugs and sat at right angles to Johnny, not meeting his eye.

"We need to know about her frame of mind," he said. "I'm sorry to have to ask, but do you think there's a chance she might have been suicidal?"

Natasha poured two mugs of tea. She looked up at him briefly, holding out a sugar bowl. Johnny shook his head. She placed a mug in front of him. It was brightly coloured with rainbow spots.

Was she going to answer the question?

He sat back and slurped his tea, watching her over the rim of the mug. She poured her own cup and shuffled into her chair, her body language uneasy.

She let out a long breath. "She was... She wasn't quite herself."

Johnny sipped more tea. It was hot. It was good.

"In what way?" he asked.

A shrug. "She rang in sick. She spoke to Bernard, that's my husband, told him she had a stomach bug."

"When was this?" Johnny asked.

"Yesterday morning," she said. "About half past six, I think."

"And that was the first day she rang in sick?"

"Yes." Natasha slurped at her tea, still not meeting his eye.

"Had she shown any signs of illness the day before?"

Natasha looked at him. "I didn't see her the day before. I hadn't seen her for a few days."

"You're her manager, aren't you?"

"That doesn't mean I see her every day. She spends most of her time over at the lagoon, I tend to be up in the woods. I'm mainly working on the conservation side of things. But she's got a team who help with maintaining the reed beds."

Johnny nodded. He had no idea what that would entail.

"So is there anybody else who would be able to tell me about her state of mind?" he asked. "Anybody who was working with her?"

"Mostly she was working with volunteers," Natasha replied. "None of them are here now. I can get you their names though, or at least Ed can. Have you met Ed?"

"He brought us over from Poole."

"Ed's alright, he's a good boss."

Johnny smiled, thinking of his own bosses. Dennis, and then the DCI. Dennis he'd known since he was not much more than a kid. The DCI, he was just getting to know. But she'd shown concern when he'd felt ill on the boat. Maybe she was worried he couldn't do his job, or perhaps she cared about how he was feeling. It didn't matter either way.

"I'll get that list," he said. "But it would be helpful if you could tell me if she was having any problems. Were there any issues between her and other members of the team? Any family troubles, relationships?"

Natasha shook her head briskly. "Simone was single. No husband, no kids, no boyfriend, as far as I know. She didn't fall out with anybody, she wasn't that sort of woman. She was easy, Simone was. Turned up in the morning, always five minutes early. Got her job done with a smile. Brilliant with the volunteers, motivated them really well."

"So she enjoyed her job?" Johnny asked.

"Loved it," said Natasha. She met his eye properly for the first time. "We all do. It's a privilege to work on this island, especially when you live here, too."

"Do you live here with your husband?" Johnny asked her.

She nodded. "Bernard's a freelance journalist, works from upstairs in the spare room."

Her gaze went up to the ceiling.

"Is he there now?" Johnny asked.

A small nod. "Sometimes he goes over to Poole chasing a story, talking to an editor. But generally he works out of this cottage."

"That must be strange," Johnny said. "Everybody else here works for the National Trust, their job involves the island."

She sipped her tea. "He never complains."

Johnny wondered if Bernard was really as happy as his wife claimed, living here surrounded by National Trust stuff, cut off from the mainland where he would find it easier to work. But it was Natasha who'd gone down to the beach with Frankie and Adam. Natasha who'd seen the body.

"So tell me about yesterday evening," Johnny said. "I've been told that Frankie Quinn knocked on your door, after finding Simone."

Natasha nodded, looking down at the table. "We had a team meeting," she said. "Me, Frankie, Anya. Simone didn't come. I just assumed it was because of the tummy bug." She sipped her tea, her eyes glazed. "I wish I'd checked."

Johnny gave her an encouraging smile. "Did anything happen at this meeting?"

"Just the usual," she sighed. "Frankie left at about ten o'clock, a little bit before, and then twenty minutes later she came back. She had Adam with her, her boyfriend. They were panicking, shouting about Simone."

"They'd found her?" Johnny asked.

Natasha cleared her throat, then wiped at her eye. "Yeah."

"And what did you do?"

"I didn't believe them." Natasha looked up. "I felt I should take charge, check what was happening. So I made them take me down to the beach. I shouldn't have, I know. I should have left well alone."

Johnny wondered how much damage they'd done. Gail would be there now, grumbling about members of the public trampling all over her crime scene.

"Did you get close to Simone?" he asked Natasha.

Natasha gave him a slow nod. "I knelt down by her. I wanted to check if she had a pulse."

"And did she?"

"No. She was pale, grey in the darkness. Her eyes, they…" She closed her own eyes. "They stared up at the clouds, it was, oh it was horrible."

She turned away, her shoulders hunched.

"It's OK," Johnny said. "You've had a shock."

Natasha turned back to him. "Sorry. You don't need me to be like this, you've got questions you need answering."

"It's not easy finding a body."

"No." Her eyes were wet.

"And then you came back here straight afterwards?"

"We did. Bernard had already rung for the coastguard, he said they were on their way."

"So do you have to call the coastguard out a lot over here?"

"No, we look after ourselves. We've got our own boats. We know better than to mess around on the water, people are well drilled on safety. Particularly those of us who live here."

Johnny nodded. "So how was your relationship with Simone?"

Natasha gripped the handle of her mug. There were dark circles beneath her eyes. "I didn't see much of her between team meetings, but we got on well. She was a good team member. Enthusiastic, well motivated, she kept people happy."

"And you enjoyed working with her?"

"I don't know what you're trying to imply?"

Johnny heard the door opening behind him. A heavily built man with thinning grey hair stood in the doorway.

"Who are you?" he asked.

Johnny stood up. "DC Chiles, Dorset Police."

The man grunted. "You here about Simone?"

"I am," Johnny replied.

"Nice girl," the man said. "Doesn't deserve it, whatever happened to her."

Johnny looked at the man's face. He seemed drawn and had deep crow's feet around his eyes.

"You're a freelance journalist?" Johnny asked him. "You don't work for the National Trust."

"No such luck," the man said. "I'm the muggins who has to go across on the ferry every other day. Running errands, grubbing for what little work I can get, that kind of thing. I look after Natasha here, let her get on with her job."

Natasha had gone very still in her chair. Johnny wondered what was going on between this couple, if they'd had an argument before he'd arrived.

The boss would want an update. They didn't need to ask anybody for alibis until they had a time of death.

He stood up. "Thanks for your time," he said. "I'll be back if I've got any more questions."

"I'm sure you will," said Bernard, his voice tight.

He stood back to let Johnny pass and opened the front door for him. Johnny walked out into the bright sunshine. The sun glinted off the harbour and a boat was passing silently.

He turned back to the front door. He opened his mouth, about to thank the couple for their time. But instead, a blank blue door stared back at him.

He hoped everybody on this island wasn't as unfriendly as the Williams.

CHAPTER THIRTEEN

Lesley left the pathologist and approached Ed Rogers. So now she had a murder to investigate. She shivered as a light breeze hit the back of her neck.

Ed was looking grim. One hand was plunged in his pocket, the other played with the National Trust fleece lanyard around his neck.

"What's the verdict?" he asked her.

She eyed him.

"We need to do a post-mortem," she said. "To confirm cause of death. But it's looking like someone did this to her."

He opened his mouth and tugged at his lower lip. "Poor Simone."

"Did you know her well?"

"As well as any of the full-time staff here." He shook his head. "Not that well, no."

"Did you see her in the last few days?"

He shook his head. "Sorry. Natasha Williams will be more use to you than I can."

"Yes."

Ed scratched his chin. "I'll make sure people know." He looked at her, blinking. "They need to know there could be a killer on the island."

"Let's not get people too alarmed just yet."

"Alarmed? They might be at risk."

Lesley took a step towards him. Nine times out of ten, a murder victim had been killed by a relative or friend. There was more chance one of Ed's staff would be arrested, than that they would be the next victim.

"Please," she said. "Let us conduct some interviews first."

He frowned. "I don't see why…" He nodded. "OK. But I'll be calling a staff meeting this evening."

"What time?"

He sniffed. "Seven."

"OK." So they had until seven before people started lying to them. "I'll help you with that."

He looked at her as if the idea hadn't occurred to him. "Of course."

"I'd like to interview all of your employees, and possibly the John Lewis folks too."

"Yes." He stared towards the beach, where Simone's body still lay.

The pathology assistants were preparing to move her. They needed to take the body somewhere where no more damage could be done to her.

Lesley pointed out to sea. "What are the currents like around here?"

Ed squinted towards the water. "Certain times of day there's a strong current flowing from Purbeck. It washes along the beaches on this side of the island, as the tide's coming in."

"So she could have been dumped in the harbour, pushed off a boat or something?" Lesley asked.

It looked like Simone had been assaulted before she'd gone in the water. But there were signs of drowning. Maybe there'd been a struggle, and she'd been pushed in. They'd know more after the post-mortem.

Lesley heard a whistle. She turned to see Whittaker summoning one of his assistants. What would it be like to work for the man, she wondered.

The two assistants bent and picked up Simone's body, encased in a body bag. They moved it further up the beach and laid it down carefully. They would be waiting for a boat to take it off the island as quickly as possible.

Ed was watching. "There are plenty of secluded spots over there on Purbeck," he said. "You've got the Arne nature reserve. And then past that, all the way up to Shell Bay there's nothing. Footpaths, wildlife, sandbanks. It can be treacherous if you don't know the area. She could have come from over there."

"You think she fell into the water on that side?" Lesley asked him.

If she had fallen in, it would be more likely she'd been here, on the island. Or in a boat on the harbour. And that didn't account for the bruising.

"What's the depth of the water on the quay we came in on?" she asked him.

"Pretty deep," he said.

"And the currents?"

He thought. "Again, depends on the time of day and the tides. A body dumped off there *could* be washed around this side of the island."

"But?"

"It would be more likely she'd wash into the lagoon."

"What's that?"

"It's to the north of the quay. Our best habitat for bird species."

"So where is she most likely to have come from, given that she was found here?"

He wrinkled his brow. "In the harbour, really. A boat."

Lesley didn't want to take Ed's word for this. She'd ask Mike to research the tidal movements, the currents washing onto this beach. They needed to know where Simone had most likely been pushed into the water.

"I need to know who's used your boats in the last few days."

"Of course. We keep a log."

"Thanks. Are they all accounted for now?"

"They are," he said. "We've got two. There's the flat-bottomed boat your CSI team brought their gear over on, and the small passenger boat that you came in on."

"I need those logs as soon as possible."

He tipped her a mock salute and walked away up the hill.

Lesley wondered how wise it was to involve this man, especially before she had firm evidence. But she had to trust somebody.

Gail trudged up the beach, her feet sinking in the soft sand.

"We're going to be here a while, Lesley," she said. "I've got a police boat coming in so we can examine the water in the vicinity. See if we can pick up any scraps of clothing, anything she or her assailant might have dropped."

"Have your team searched Simone's house yet?"

"Brett's nearly done. She kept the place tidy. Nothing out of the ordinary."

"OK. Keep me posted," Lesley told her.

"Will do." Gail turned back to the beach and called to Gav.

Lesley stared out to sea, wondering what Simone had done to deserve such a fate. Half-strangled and then drowned. It was like somebody wanted to kill her twice over.

CHAPTER FOURTEEN

Johnny was on the other side of the church as Lesley approached it. She gave him a wave to attract his attention. Grey clouds blocked the sun but it was still warm. She perched on a wall outside the church and waited.

"Alright, boss," he said.

"You look a bit healthier," she told him.

He shrugged. "Seasickness has worn off." He looked towards the quay, clearly not looking forward to the journey back.

"We might need to stay here," she said.

"Stay here?" He looked perturbed.

"I don't relish the thought of going back and forth across the harbour every day," she told him. "If we can get ourselves a room in that castle for a couple of days, we can get any interviews done quickly and be on hand if Gail's team turn up any forensics."

He gave her a long look, as if considering whether or not to object. "Fair enough, boss," he said. "I'll have to ring my wife."

Lesley knew that Johnny had a young wife at home. She couldn't remember the woman's name.

"Have you got kids?" she asked him.

"One on the way." He smiled, his eyes dancing. "Due in September."

"No chance of it coming earlier?"

"Due date's September the seventh. Five weeks to go. To be honest, I think she'll appreciate having me out of her hair for a few days. She's been a bit…" He caught Lesley's expression and tailed off.

"Be patient with her, Johnny. It's not easy carrying another human being around inside you. Especially in this heat."

Johnny wiped his forehead as if only just noticing the temperature. "Yeah. I'm sure she'll be fine with it. Saves me having to take too many boat trips." He grinned.

Saves me watching you look like you're about to puke all over me too, Lesley thought. "Good," she said. "I'll see if they've got a room we can use."

"A room?" Johnny's eyes widened.

Lesley gave him a mock punch on the arm. "One each, Johnny. There's no way we're bunking up together."

He breathed out, relieved. Budgets were tight, but she doubted that he'd really expected to have to share with her.

It would be an opportunity to get to know him better. He seemed to hide behind Dennis when they were in the office. She wanted to know what made him tick. Whether he had potential to go further, despite eight years as a DC.

"So," she said. "Who have you spoken to?"

"The couple who found the body," he told her. "Frankie Quinn and Adam Stanley."

"And how did that go?"

"Their stories match up," he said. "I spoke to them separately. She was at a team meeting at her manager's house. Natasha Williams."

"Have you spoken to her?"

"I have. It was her husband who made the call to the coastguard."

"What's the timeline?"

69

He checked his notes again. "The meeting broke up at around quarter to ten. Frankie Quinn left just after ten, her partner Adam was waiting outside for her. They went for a walk down to the beach, found the body."

Lesley shivered. "Did they disturb her?"

Johnny shook his head. "Both of them say they didn't. They went back to the Williams house and brought Natasha Williams back down to the beach with them."

"Why?" Lesley asked.

He shrugged. "It seems Natasha wanted to see for herself before she made the call."

Lesley didn't like that. "Why would you do that? Surely every second they can gain in calling the emergency services…"

"Natasha couldn't account for why she did it. Says she knows she was being illogical. But she got her husband to make the call, while she was gone."

So Natasha Williams had believed Frankie Quinn sufficiently to call the emergency services, but still wanted to see the body for herself. Lesley filed that away as something she needed to follow up.

"Right," she said. "So did any of them tell you when they last saw Simone?"

"Natasha saw her on Friday," Johnny replied. "Simone took yesterday off sick, rang Natasha's house, spoke to her husband."

"Whose husband?"

"Natasha's husband, Bernard. She told him she wasn't feeling well, didn't come out of her cottage all day."

"Was anyone else there? At the meeting?"

He nodded. "Anya Davinski, the other member of the team. She left in between Frankie leaving and her and Adam returning. And she says she saw Simone on Monday night."

"You've spoken to her?"

"Yes, boss. Just talked to her. They met for a drink outside the café by the quay."

"The café was open?"

He shook his head. "Anya said they sit there when it's closed. There's tables. She's got a key to the garden, it's a good place to watch the water. Apparently."

"And what time did Simone go home?"

"About nine."

"They walk together?"

"Simone left Anya at the café. Locking up."

"Where does Anya live?"

"Opposite direction." He pointed towards the quay. "One of the cottages by the water."

Simone would have been walking up this way, past the church. If she'd been attacked, Anya wouldn't have seen. Unless Anya was lying.

"OK," she said. "So we've got Anya being the last person to see her alive, Bernard Williams the last person to speak to her. Did you believe them?"

"No reason not to."

She eyed him. There was plenty reason not to.

"I want to know if anyone saw Simone on Tuesday, after she rang in sick. And if she was seen with Anya, on Monday night."

"We can ask around."

Lesley sighed. "Uniform are bringing more people in. There are forty-two people here, you and I can't cover them all."

"We need to cover them all?"

"Any of them could be a witness. I'd rather go to them than wait for them to approach us after they've all conferred."

Lesley peered past Johnny, towards the farm buildings. Beyond there she knew Gail was working hard, trying to find as much evidence as she could before the tide washed it away. A body washed up on a tidal shore was far from ideal, but if anybody was going to find clues for her, it would be Gail.

"OK," she said. "So Ed Rogers has told me he's working on a list of visitors who've been here, National Trust members at least. And we've already got a list of the staff on the island, National Trust and John Lewis. I want to talk to the John Lewis manager. We need to know who saw Simone, if anybody had contact with her after Monday night."

"Yes, boss," he said.

"Talk to Ed," she said. "Get a map of the island, work your way round those houses methodically. Let's take advantage of the fact that people are stuck inside, not out working."

"No problem."

"And we'll have more people here soon. Tina's going to be over on the next boat, along with some uniform."

Johnny looked relieved. "So maybe we won't need to stay over?"

She wasn't so sure. Truth was, she wanted to keep an eye on the people living on this island while the investigation was ongoing. "We'll be as quick as we can, Johnny. Don't you worry."

She put a hand on his shoulder as she stood up. Her skirt was dirty from the wall. "Let me know if you get anything helpful, yes?"

"No problem, boss."

CHAPTER FIFTEEN

As Lesley turned away from Johnny and headed towards the quay, she spotted a familiar figure in a Dorset Police uniform walking towards her. She approached PC Tina Abbott, smiling.

"Tina," she said. "That was quick."

Tina gave her a satisfied shrug. "We came by police boat, there are three more uniformed PCs with me."

"Nice work," said Lesley. She turned to beckon Johnny over. He gave Tina a smile which she returned.

"OK," said Lesley. "I need the five of you to divvy up the people who work on this island. Start with National Trust staff. I'll speak to the manager of the John Lewis lot."

"No problem, boss," said Tina.

She pulled a sheet of paper out of her inside pocket. "I've brought a full list of staff…"

"I've already got that," Johnny said.

"…along with an organisation structure and a list of who lives in which house."

Johnny visibly deflated. "Nice work," he muttered. Tina gave him an awkward smile.

Lesley felt some of the tension ease out of her. It was good to have somebody efficient arrive.

"I'll leave you to it," Lesley told them. It wasn't her job to make sure they got along.

"What do you want us to ask them?" Tina asked.

"Johnny?" Lesley said.

"Simone, that's our victim, she was last seen on Monday night by her colleague Anya Davinski. We want to know if anyone else saw her after that, or if they saw the two of them together. And anything about Simone's relationships with the other people here. Who might have wanted her dead."

Tina winced. "Got it."

"Good," said Lesley. "Let me know how you get on."

She turned away and passed three uniformed officers, all men, who were rounding the wall next to the castle. They each ma'amed her in turn and she nodded in response.

Lesley turned to see Tina and Johnny conferring with the three officers, giving them their instructions. Tina looked to be holding her own. *Good for her.* When she'd started in the Major Crimes team, she'd behaved like an imposter, paranoid that Dennis in particular would never accept her. But she'd spent the last two months proving herself, and now here she was, ordering her colleagues in uniform around. Maybe she'd apply for CID one day.

The officers peeled off and walked away in separate directions. Hopefully, these interviews could be conducted quickly. Maybe Johnny would be able to go home to his wife tonight after all.

No. Lesley wanted him with her at the 7pm staff meeting.

But first, she needed to speak to Yolanda Harte, the woman Ed had told her managed the John Lewis staff here. From what she'd seen, it didn't look like the John Lewis and National Trust teams had much contact with each other, but that didn't mean that there wasn't a connection.

She walked towards the tall brick wall that surrounded the castle. It was imposing, forbidding. *Keep out*, it said, despite the lack of any signs.

As Lesley approached, a high black gate in the wall opened and a woman emerged. She was tall and thin with short blonde hair, wearing a blue suit. She was the first person Lesley had seen not wearing a National Trust uniform.

The woman walked up towards the farm buildings, taking a short cut across the grass and ignoring Lesley. Somewhere in the distance, that damn peacock wailed.

Lesley hesitated. If the woman was making for the beach…

As the woman approached the farm buildings, Ed Rogers appeared from beyond. He stopped when he reached the woman.

Lesley watched as the two of them fell into conversation. They spoke for a moment, then the atmosphere changed.

Ed was gesticulating, his head jerking, his skin reddening. The woman had planted her feet slightly apart and had her hands on her hips. Her back was to Lesley.

Lesley squinted. Who was this woman and why was Ed so annoyed with her? Was he trying to keep her away from the crime scene?

Lesley shifted sideways, towards the wall. She could vaguely hear Ed's voice, but couldn't make out the words. The woman was shouting at him, her voice high-pitched and shrill. Whatever it was, this pair weren't happy with each other.

After a few more moments, the woman stamped her foot and turned angrily away from Ed. He stood with his hands on his hips, watching as she walked back towards Lesley.

Lesley straightened as the woman approached. Most people would turn away, pretend not to have been listening. But Lesley was a copper. It was her job to listen.

As the woman spotted her, her steps slowed. Her hair was messed up, she'd been tugging at it as she walked. What had happened to annoy this woman so much? Was she connected to Simone?

As the woman neared Lesley, she stopped and gave her a haughty look. "Who are you?"

Lesley met the woman's stare. "DCI Clarke. Dorset Police."

The woman shifted backwards. "Oh." She frowned, then started to walk past Lesley, altering her route to give Lesley a wide berth.

"And who are you?" Lesley called out as the woman was about to pass her.

The woman stopped walking, her heels almost skidding in the gravel. "Yolanda Harte," she said. "I manage the John Lewis hotel."

CHAPTER SIXTEEN

Lesley was about to follow the woman, intrigued to know why she'd been arguing with Ed, when her phone rang.

Damn.

The woman glanced back, having heard Lesley's phone.

Lesley grabbed her phone from her pocket. "What is it?" she snapped, watching the woman hurry away. She eased the tall gates to the castle open and slipped inside, pulling them shut behind her. Lesley had no doubt she'd locked them, too.

"Sorry," said Dennis. "I've got something you need to know about."

Lesley put her hand to her head and dug her fingernails into her scalp. "What, Dennis? What's so urgent?"

"You OK, boss?" he asked.

"I'm fine," she replied. "Just tell me why you're calling."

She stared at the closed gates. That couldn't be the only way into the castle.

"It's the press," Dennis said. "Mike just had a journalist on the phone. Sadie Dawes."

"I know that name."

"She's the one who reported on Harry Nevin's death. She's a terrier."

Lesley had nothing against terriers, except when they derailed her investigations. And she knew how disruptive a tenacious journalist could be.

She sighed. "It had to happen eventually."

"She's heading over there," Dennis told her. "Told us she was ringing as a courtesy."

"Oh, that's very courteous of her," she replied. "But no boats are coming in or out of this island."

"She's hired a private boat," he said. "I wouldn't be surprised if she moored up on one of the beaches."

Lesley came to a stop on the path, her body thrumming with anger. "She's done *what*?"

"Sorry, boss," Dennis replied, his voice subdued. "Just wanted to let you know."

Lesley turned to look back where Ed Rogers had disappeared. After his argument with Yolanda Harte, he'd gone round the back of the church. Was he inside? She needed his help with this, not to mention those uniformed officers, now busily knocking on doors.

"OK," she said to Dennis. "Have you got any inform-ation about what kind of boat this might be?"

"Sorry, boss," he said. "Just thought I'd warn you."

"Thanks." She sighed. "I appreciate it."

"How's it going over there?"

"Slow," she replied. "I get the feeling not everyone here is on speaking terms."

"Isolated community. Can get a bit nasty."

She shook her head, looking around her. The grassy area in front of the church was empty, a few hens waddling around, clucking quietly. The place seemed so peaceful. What had led to a woman being murdered here?

"I'll call you later," she said. "Have you got any back-ground for me? Anything on Simone?"

"Mike's checking her background," Dennis told her. "But there's nothing of any interest yet."

"No record? No criminal connections?"

It was a long shot, she knew.

"Nothing."

That was what she'd been expecting. It made it all the more likely her killer was here on the island.

"We found her next of kin, though," Dennis said. "Her parents, they live in Southampton."

Lesley closed her eyes. She pictured the state of the body on the beach, the bloating and foaming at the mouth. Hopefully Whittaker would do a good job of cleaning Simone up before her parents came to formally identify her.

"OK," she said to Dennis. "Make contact with them, set up the appointment."

"Already on it, boss," he said.

"Is that everything?"

"Yes. Sorry to interrupt. You in the middle of something?"

"I just need to follow up on an argument I just witnessed."

CHAPTER SEVENTEEN

Gail surveyed the passenger boat moored to the quay below her feet. It bobbed up and down on the water, reminding her of what Lesley had told her about Johnny. Poor guy, she thought. Not the best assignment to be drafted in on when you suffered from seasickness.

Gav appeared behind her, lugging an equipment bag. "We checking this one first?"

She looked past this boat towards the flat-bottomed one they'd come in on. It was attached to a buoy further out. "We can use this one to get to that one, I suppose."

"Assuming it's clean."

"Of course."

"Let's get started, then."

He clambered down into the boat, easy enough with him being six-foot-five, and held up a hand to guide her in. Gail was short, heavier than she'd like to be. She had the kind of body that wasn't suited to clambering in and out of boats.

She stood in the centre of the boat, surveying the structure. This boat had been used since Simone had been found on Tuesday night. Lesley and Johnny had come in on it. But prior to that, it hadn't been used since Sunday afternoon. That was something, she supposed. Lesley hadn't mentioned anything untoward about it. It was unlikely they'd find anything, but they had to cover all bases.

"You start that end," she told Gav, pointing towards the bow of the boat. "I'll start at the back. We'll work our way inwards, cover every surface."

Gav gave her a nod and climbed over the seats to the front of the boat. Gail made her way to the stern, starting with the outside of the boat. She leaned over, holding onto the rail. She examined the area around the motor, looking for anything Simone or her attacker might have left behind. Strands of hair, fragments of clothing. There was nothing.

She took photos as she went, planting her feet firmly in the boat, her legs wide apart. The last thing she needed was to fall in, especially with this camera being worth a small fortune.

After she'd checked the back of the boat inside and out, she moved on to the rear seat. It spanned the width of the boat and was made of moulded plastic. She examined its surface, kneeling down and using her camera to zoom in and get a better view.

It was clean, the surface scoured by sea water. Gail groaned as Gav moved behind her and the boat tipped to one side.

"Careful, mate," she muttered.

"Sorry, Gail. I'll be more careful."

"You do that."

She bent over to see beneath the seat, but it was difficult without losing her balance. Instead she turned her camera and held it out, under the seat, pointing upwards. She moved the camera slowly along the underside of the seat, firing off photos as she went. When she reached the other side of the boat, she lifted the camera and checked the screen. On the third photograph, she squinted.

"Hang on a minute," she said.

"You got something?" Gav asked.

She didn't turn to look at him. Instead, she flicked through to the next photograph, which overlapped this one.

"I think I might do," she said.

Aw, hell. She would have to get under there.

"Gav, I need you to sit up there but stay very still. I'm going to have to get right down in the bottom of this boat."

She twisted herself so she was on her back and all but lying in the bottom of the boat, her head beneath the seat. She peered up.

"I can't see anything," she said. "Pass me a torch, will you?"

She reached a hand out, blindly taking the torch Gav placed in it. She pulled it close to her face and shone it up at the surface above. The floor was damp, water swishing from side to side. Her hair was getting wet. Filthy too, probably. She'd regret this later.

She worked along the underside of the seat with the torch until she found what she'd seen in the photo.

"Got it."

She lifted her head to get a better look, then dropped down again and raised the camera to her eye. She fired off a few more photos, struggling to focus in the confined space. Eventually, she managed to struggle out and stand up again. Gav was watching her, his movements small, anxious not to make the boat topple.

"What have you got?" he asked.

She took a few deep breaths. She felt light-headed; she'd been holding her breath.

"Blood," she told him. "There's blood under this seat and it's relatively fresh."

CHAPTER EIGHTEEN

Lesley put her phone away and turned back towards the castle.

She had to speak to that woman. She wanted to know why she'd been arguing with Ed and whether it was connected to Simone's death.

She strode towards the gates and pushed them. Nothing. There was no handle, no latch for her to grab hold of. She pushed her fingers into the gap between the gates and tried to pull.

Again, nothing. There had to be another way into that castle.

She walked towards the quay. There was a shop down here, and a café. The people who worked in them would either be on the mainland or tucked away in their houses, instructed to stay put by Ed. But it was worth a try. The café was on the right as she approached the quay. She turned down a path leading to it and pushed at the door.

Nothing.

She pulled back and looked over the low building towards the castle.

There was another gate around the side of the cafe. She went to it and knocked. Still no answer.

Bloody hell, this is ridiculous. They had to let people in somehow.

She skirted back to the gates she'd already tried and checked again for some sort of intercom or buzzer.

Bingo. She'd missed it the first time, hidden in ivy that climbed up the wall.

She pressed the button. After a few moments, a voice crackled over the intercom.

"Hello?"

"My name is DCI Clarke. I'm investigating a suspicious death on the island. I need to speak to Yolanda Harte."

"Sorry, who?"

"Yolanda Harte. I'm told she manages—"

"No. Who are you?"

Lesley pushed down irritation. "DCI Clarke, Dorset Police. Let me in, please."

"Oh." A pause. "Hang on a minute."

Lesley waited. After a few moments she heard movement behind the gate and at last it opened. A short woman in a grey uniform stood beyond it, giving her a wary look. This wasn't the woman who'd argued with Ed.

"I'm Greta, I manage reception. You can talk to me."

Lesley raised her badge. "Like I say, I need to speak to the hotel manager."

The woman tightened her lips and turned towards the castle. It was even more imposing close up, staring out to sea like a fortress. A broad garden led down to the waterfront, manicured flower beds and neat paths. People strolled between trees near the water, and a man sat in a sun lounger on a terrace next to the building. So the John Lewis staff hadn't been told to stay indoors. But still, they were all imprisoned in here, thought Lesley, in their luxurious compound.

She followed the woman into the building and a wide hallway. Wooden stairs swept up ahead of her. The walls were panelled to waist level, with ornate wallpaper above. The carpet beneath her feet was plush. Someone had spent a lot of money on the upkeep of this place.

"Wait here, please." The woman turned and disappeared through a door.

Lesley folded her arms and tapped her foot on the carpet. She checked her watch. Two o'clock. She hoped Tina and Johnny were making progress with those witness statements.

At last the door opened and the tall blonde woman she'd seen with Ed emerged. The woman cocked her head as she saw Lesley.

"You're the one who was watching me with Ed Rogers."

"I am." Lesley held up her badge. "DCI Clarke, Dorset Police. I imagine you know why I'm here."

"Terrible business," the woman said.

She held out a skinny hand and Lesley took it. The woman's handshake was limp and half-hearted.

"Come into my office," Yolanda said. "You can update me on your investigation."

Lesley was about to say that wasn't why she was here, when the woman turned to retreat down a broad corridor.

Lesley followed, disgruntled at the unease this woman made her feel.

CHAPTER NINETEEN

Gail stood to one side to let Gav pass. She shuffled towards the front of the boat, careful to keep her movements steady, and sat down on one of the benches, checking it first to be sure she wasn't contaminating evidence.

Given Gav's height, it wasn't easy for him to fold himself into the confined space, but he somehow managed an origami-like move and squeezed himself in.

"We'll need to remove this bench," he said. "Only way to get that blood off."

Gail nodded. "Have we got the cutting equipment with us?"

He unfolded himself and stood up. "Not here, but it's on the island. That Ed bloke let me use a storeroom."

"He's very helpful, isn't he?" Gail said.

Gav reached up behind his neck and massaged the muscles, screwing his face up as he did so. "You think it's suspicious?"

Gail wrinkled her nose. The problem with this job was that you started to suspect everybody of being fishy. Even a bloke who was just being nice.

"Nah," she said. "Ignore me."

Stop being paranoid. And she wasn't even one of the detectives.

"OK," she continued. "You go and get the kit. I'll examine the area around that seat before we do any damage. Check there isn't anything else."

"We need to let the National Trust know we're wrecking their boat."

"Shit." The CSI team were perfectly entitled to damage property, if it meant uncovering forensic evidence. Gail knew teams who didn't bother with even the basics of putting things together afterwards. But as far as she was concerned, it was about respect, and cooperation. If she didn't do people the basic courtesy of leaving their property in the best state she could, how could she expect their cooperation?

She searched under the seat and in its vicinity, using a torch and then a UV light. There was nothing else. Just that patch of blood. It was smeared. She hoped there would be prints, but couldn't make any out.

Lesley needed to know about this. The blood was a reddish-brown. Not the bright red of fresh blood. But not the rusty brown of a very old stain, either. It had been left within the last few days.

Gail clambered out of the boat, glad no one could see her making an absolute hash of it. She stood on the edge of the quay, panting, thinking for the hundredth time this month that she needed to get fit.

She dialled. The phone rang out twice and clicked into voicemail.

"Lesley," Gail said into the phone as she saw Gav approaching. He was carrying a case with the cutting kit and had Ed Rogers with him. Ed didn't look happy. "We've found blood on the National Trust's boat. It could be Simone's."

She thought back to the state of the body. A drowned body had its secrets, but she hadn't seen blood.

She took a breath as Gav and Ed reached her. She raised a hand: *just a moment*.

"Or it could be her attacker's," she breathed into the phone.

CHAPTER TWENTY

Yolanda Harte's office was a grand room at the rear of the building. Tall sash windows looked over a copse of trees and the sea off to one side.

Lesley took one of the two chairs opposite the desk, while Yolanda sat behind it. She placed her elbows on the desk and eyed Lesley.

"So you'll be wanting to talk to our partners as well, I imagine."

"I want to speak to you to start with. Tell me how closely the two teams mix. Do you have much contact with the National Trust people?"

Yolanda shook her head. "We keep ourselves to ourselves, really. We've got our own boat. We bring the partners over on changeover days."

"Changeover days?"

"Fridays and Mondays. That's when people come and go. Today's a Wednesday, and Head Office have told me to clear the place out. It's not going to be easy. But some of our guests are pretty spooked."

"I'd like to speak with your guests and staff before anyone leaves."

"You'll have to be quick."

Lesley placed a hand on the desk. "Ms Harte, this is a murder investigation. Anyone staying on this island could be a witness. Or a suspect."

Yolanda pursed her lips. She opened a desk drawer, and pulled out a sheet of paper which she placed on the desk between them.

"A list of the partners living here." She pointed to a list of people at the top of the sheet, then moved her finger down. "Staff living on the mainland who've been on duty this week." She turned the sheet over. "And current guests."

"Are they all here now?"

"They are. We'll be using the boat later, sending guests home first."

"Not just yet," said Lesley. She took the sheet of paper. She would ask Mike to run these names against the HOLMES database.

Yolanda shrugged. "Not much I can do to stop it," she said. "But you'll find our people have got nothing to do with all this."

Lesley raised an eyebrow. "Let's not make assumptions."

Lesley knew that it was more likely Simone's killer was one of her National Trust colleagues. But she couldn't imagine that on an island with a permanent population of just forty-two, the two groups didn't mingle.

The potential suspect list was like an onion. The team Simone worked within at the centre, the next layer the National Trust staff. Outside that, the John Lewis staff, and then the outer edge, the hundreds of visitors who'd been here over the last two days.

They needed to narrow it down.

Lesley picked up the sheet of paper, folded it, and put it in her inside pocket, just as her phone rang. She pulled it out and hit the button to reject the call. Whoever it was, they could wait.

"Can you tell me what you were arguing with Ed Rogers about before?"

Yolanda straightened in her chair. "I don't know what you're talking about."

"I saw you up by the church, about fifteen minutes ago. You were clearly having a heated discussion about something."

Yolanda shook her head. "I saw Ed, sure. He was updating me on what you people were doing."

You people.

Lesley thought of Yolanda's body language when she'd been talking to Ed. The way she'd stormed off, Ed's wild gesticulations as he spoke. There was no way that had been a friendly update.

"Is there often conflict between the two groups on the island?" she asked.

Yolanda leaned forwards, clenching her fists on the desk. "You're making up stories where none exist," she said. "Just because a woman has died here, doesn't mean there's conflict between my team and hers. We get along fine. We have very different roles and we live side by side here. Nothing more to it than that."

Lesley wasn't convinced. There was clearly no love lost between this woman and Ed Rogers, and she wanted to know why.

CHAPTER TWENTY-ONE

Johnny was walking from the direction of the church when Lesley emerged from the castle.

Yolanda Harte's attitude had left a nasty taste in her mouth. The woman was keen to get her guests and staff off the island, to shield them from the tragedy of Simone Browning's death, and that seemed fair enough. But when Lesley saw that kind of agitation on someone, her copper senses began to tingle.

"How far have you got?" she asked Johnny as he hurried towards her.

Johnny shook his head. "I've spoken to four people so far. Just called Tina and she's on her third. This is going to take a while."

Lesley nodded. She checked her watch: five forty-five. Either those uniformed PCs would need to be sent home soon, or she'd need to have a conversation with Detective Superintendent Carpenter about overtime. She knew that budgets here were even tighter than they had been in the West Midlands.

Her phone buzzed: a text from Gail.

"Damn." She'd forgotten about the call while she'd been in with Yolanda. "Hang on a minute, Johnny."

Lesley checked the text.

> Forensics found on boat. Call me.

She looked at Johnny, knowing her face had lit up.

"We've got something," she told him.

"What?"

She didn't respond, already busy dialling Gail.

"Lesley, I've been trying to get hold of you."

"Sorry. I was interviewing someone. What have you found?"

"Blood, on the underside of the seat at the back of the boat. The one you and Johnny came in on. I estimate it's recent, but more than a few hours old."

Lesley covered her phone with her hand. "Johnny, there's no chance you could have left blood on that boat, is there?"

"Which boat?"

"The National Trust boat. The one we came in on."

He frowned. "No, boss." He wrinkled his forehead, no doubt remembering how he'd felt on the trip.

Lesley didn't have any cuts herself and hadn't seen any on Ed, so she didn't see how the blood could have come from any of them.

She removed her hand from the phone. "Check it out, Gail. It could be relevant."

"Already on it. Gav's going to cut that seat away from the structure. We've got Ed with us. He's not best pleased, but there's nothing we can do."

"I want the whole boat impounded," Lesley said. "Not just that seat. If it was used to take Simone out onto the harbour…"

"Right-o. Leave it with me." Gail hung up.

Lesley looked at Johnny. "You know where Tina is now?"

"I can call her."

"Do that. I want to get an update. They've given us use of a room off the café. I'll call Dennis too, get him on speaker."

"You want Tina's Uniform mates in on it too?"

"No. They've got an hour or so to cover as many people as they can before that staff meeting. I'll get Carpenter to agree some overtime, it's got to be better than dragging them back here again tomorrow."

"Boss."

Johnny grabbed his phone. Lesley turned towards the café.

CHAPTER TWENTY-TWO

The room in the café building was long and narrow, with a table running down the centre and a row of French doors along one side. They faced sideways to the waterfront, so you could get a view if you craned your neck.

Lesley didn't need to worry about views.

Johnny entered, Tina behind him.

Lesley turned and gave the PC a smile. "Anything to report?"

"Sorry, boss. Nobody I've spoken to saw anything suspicious on Monday night or Tuesday morning. There was one couple who knew Simone, but hadn't noticed anything odd about her lately."

"OK. You and your colleagues will need to head back to the mainland soon. Johnny and I are going to stay here overnight. You've squared it with your wife, Johnny?"

"She says it's fine. Looking forward to having more space in the bed, I bet. And they've found us a two-bedroom cottage, down past the castle."

"Cozy." Lesley wished she'd thought to bring an overnight bag with her. "Tina, if we make arrangements to get some of our things to the office, can you bring them over tomorrow?"

"Of course."

Lesley knew that logistically, the easiest option would be for Elsa to take a bag into her office and have Tina pick it up from there. But given that Elsa's law firm had been at the centre of their last murder investigation, it wasn't something she felt comfortable proposing.

"I'm going to call Dennis," she said. "Get him and Mike on speaker."

She brought up Dennis's number on her phone, then reconsidered and switched to Mike's.

"DC Legg."

"Mike, it's Lesley. Are you with Dennis?"

"Yes, boss. We were waiting till we heard from you before finishing for the day."

Good for them. "Excellent. Put me on speaker, will you?"

"One moment."

Lesley put her phone on the table and waited. Eventually Dennis's voice came over.

"We're both here."

"Good." Lesley took a seat and gestured for Johnny and Tina to do the same. This table had sixteen chairs. She wondered what it was normally used for.

"We've had a development on the forensics," she said. "Gail's found blood on the National Trust boat. She thinks it was left there in the last few days."

"Has the boat been impounded?" Dennis asked.

"She's in the process of doing that right now."

Lesley knew that Gail would have to examine the boat more thoroughly *in situ* before she could move it. And then it would have to be transported dry, which meant bringing another boat across and ferrying it over to a trailer on the mainland.

All of this would have to take place quickly, before there was further degradation of evidence. It would be a late night for Gail and her team.

"So Dennis," she said. "I want you and Mike liaising with CSI once the boat's in dry storage. Let me know if anything more comes up."

"She found anything other than blood? Hair, fibres?"

"Just blood. So far."

"Do you have suspects?"

"Not yet. Simone was part of a team of four women, one of whom found her. Frankie Quinn. Then there's Frankie's partner Adam Stanley, who was there when she found her. And the husband of Natasha, who manages the team."

"Any tensions between them? Motive?"

"It all seems hunky dory, from what they're telling us. But it could be a front. Johnny and I are going to stay here, so we can keep an eye on them."

There was a pause, then Dennis's voice came over the speaker again.

"I think that's a sensible idea. Don't you, Johnny?"

Lesley looked at Johnny, whose cheeks had high spots of pink.

"Yes, Sarge."

Dennis and Johnny had been acting oddly with each other lately. Their usual camaraderie had diminished and as far as Lesley was aware, they hadn't gone to the pub together for a few weeks.

Was that why Dennis had been so keen for Johnny to come over to the island with her? Was he trying to get rid of the DC?

"Have you unearthed anything on Simone or the people around her?" she asked.

"The woman who found her, you said that was Frankie Quinn?" Mike asked.

"It was," Lesley replied.

"She was arrested in 2008," he replied.

Lesley felt her skin prickle. "What for?"

"Assault. She tried to stab her ex. No charges were brought."

"Why not?"

"Domestic violence case. She had a restraining order against him, he breached it, she went for him with a knife."

Johnny whistled. Tina gave him a nudge and he clamped his lips shut.

"Any other arrests, previous violence?"

"Nothing in HOLMES, boss," Mike replied.

Lesley nodded. It sounded like Frankie Quinn had been provoked. If her ex had been abusing her, then she could see why the woman might react.

But it was something she needed to follow up.

"OK. Find out what happened to the ex, if he breached the order again. Where he went after that. I want to know how she ended up working here, and if there might be a connection."

"Will do."

Lesley turned at the sound of the door opening behind her. A uniformed PC with thinning red hair and a face full of freckles slid in.

"Everything OK?" Tina asked him. Lesley checked her watch: quarter past six. They needed to prepare for the staff meeting.

"You'll be wanting to get back to the mainland," she said to the male PC.

"It's not that, Ma'am." He smoothed his hands down his jacket. "I've got a witness who said she heard two women screaming at each other near the church on Monday night."

"Screaming?"

"That's what she said." He pulled out his notebook. "*Going at it hammer and tongs*, was what she told me."

"She able to tell you who these two women were?"

"They'd gone by the time she got near them, Ma'am. But she said one of them had a Yorkshire accent."

"Simone Browning was from Yorkshire," Tina said.

Lesley's mouth was dry. "Monday night. What time?"

"About nine," the PC replied.

Lesley frowned. "That's while Anya Davinski said Simone left her."

"Maybe it was Anya she was having the row with," Johnny suggested.

"Maybe. We need to talk to her again. Johnny, get over to her cottage. You know where it is."

"Boss." Johnny squeezed past the two PCs and left the room.

Lesley looked at the PC. "What's your name, Constable?"

"PC McGuigan, Ma'am."

She sighed. Carpenter had authorised overtime until 7pm, no later.

"OK, PC McGuigan. You head back on that boat with PC Abbott. I'll speak to your bosses, you'll be back here in the morning."

"Ma'am."

"And give me details of your witness. I want to speak to her before the staff meeting."

Lesley turned back to the phone once the constable had left. "Get all that?" she asked.

"Got it, boss," replied Dennis.

"Good. Now, Mike, I've got a list of names for you. People who've been staying at the castle, people who live there, people who work there but commute from the mainland. I need you to get to work on HOLMES."

"No problem, boss," said Mike. She couldn't hear a sigh or any other sign of weariness in his voice, but then, he didn't know how long the list was yet.

CHAPTER TWENTY-THREE

Frankie was washing up the dinner things when she heard a knock at the door. She and Adam had eaten early, knowing the staff meeting was planned for seven o'clock.

She checked the clock on the kitchen wall: twenty to seven. It only took five minutes to get to the admin building by the quay, where Ed would be holding the meeting.

So who was knocking on her door when they would all be there shortly?

She wiped her hands on a tea towel and went to open the door. Natasha stood on the doorstep, shifting from foot to foot.

"Frankie," she said. "How are you?"

Frankie gave her a smile. "Come in. I'm OK, considering. How are you?"

Natasha sighed as she followed Frankie through the hallway and into the kitchen. "I don't know," she said. "I feel all at sixes and sevens. Poor Simone."

Frankie let her gaze drop to the floor. She muttered agreement.

The kitchen door opened and Adam stood in the doorway, his expression serious. "Hi, Natasha," he said. "How are you?"

Natasha shrugged and lowered herself into a chair. "Just dealing with the fallout. I need to speak to her family."

Frankie felt a chill run down her back. "Parents?" she asked.

Natasha nodded. "They live in Southampton. The police have contacted them, they need her to formally identify Simone's body."

She slumped, her jaw slack. Frankie took the seat opposite her.

Natasha looked across the table at her. Her face was grey, her hair unwashed. "But I wanted to talk to them too, as her manager."

Frankie leaned over and gave Natasha a squeeze on the arm. The four of them were a tight-knit team. They often went days without seeing each other, working at opposite ends of the island. But that didn't mean they weren't close when they did see each other. The island could feel like a whole universe, and it was good to have people in it you could rely on.

Only now, one of those people had been murdered.

Natasha had been acting strangely before all this had happened. There'd been an air of unease around her, of jumpiness. Frankie had been watching her for a few weeks, trying to work out if it was something she'd done. She'd hoped Natasha didn't have plans to quit her job. She couldn't believe Natasha would ever leave this job.

Adam looked up at the clock. "You need to get going soon."

"You're not coming?" asked Frankie.

He sighed. "Can't just one of us go?"

Frankie frowned at him. "I'd rather you came too."

He nodded. "I'm just a volunteer. I wouldn't be here if I wasn't with you."

"You live on this island," Frankie told him. "You're affected by all this, and besides…" She trailed off.

They would all know what she was thinking. She and Adam had been the ones to find the body. Everybody there tonight would know that. There would be sideways glances, questions. Frankie was dreading it.

"Come with me." Her voice was hoarse. "Please."

He nodded. She gave him a tight *thank you* smile.

Frankie turned back to Natasha. "Was there a specific reason you came here first? I mean, I don't mind at all…"

Natasha shook her head. "I thought we could walk over there together."

"It's hard."

Natasha nodded.

Frankie tightened her grip on Natasha's arm. "I'm worried about you. You seem…"

"A member of our team has just died, Frankie. We're all grieving."

Frankie pulled back. "Of course." But there was more to it than that, she was sure.

She watched Natasha, her eyes narrowing. Surely her boss, her lovely boss, who didn't even feel like a boss, hadn't had anything to do with Simone's death?

Stop it. They didn't need this. They should be pulling together, not mistrusting each other.

She stood up. "Come on then."

Frankie hurried into the hall, glad to be out of the room, and grabbed her coat. There was a chill outside, the breeze from the water brushing across the island.

No one had followed her. She turned back to the kitchen door, where Adam was standing. "Let's get going."

Natasha rose from her chair, her movements careful. There was an air of distraction about her, as if she was miles away.

She would be thinking about Simone. But she'd been like this a lot lately.

Frankie eyed her friend. What was she hiding? And did it have anything to do with Simone's death?

CHAPTER TWENTY-FOUR

Lesley stood outside the address PC McGuigan had given her. Diana Berry lived in a small cottage on the southwest side of the island. It was quiet here, wind blowing across from the harbour. Lesley wondered what it must be like to live somewhere so remote. Within sight of civilisation, but a good hour from reaching it.

She knocked on the door for the second time. No answer. Maybe the woman was on her way to the staff meeting.

Her phone rang.

"DCI Clarke."

"Boss, it's Johnny." He sounded agitated.

"What's up? Are you at the staff meeting?"

"I've had a call."

"What kind of call?"

"My wife, boss."

Lesley felt her shoulders slump. "Is it the baby?"

"I don't know, boss. She said I need to get home quick as I can."

Lesley felt anxiety run through her. She knew what it was like to be carrying a baby. Sixteen years ago, but the memories were still there. That constant sense of dread in case anything went wrong. Lesley had been relieved when Terry had told her he didn't want to have another child. She'd struggled with the stress of keeping Sharon

106

safe inside her own body, of having sole responsibility for her.

"You go home," she told Johnny. "Get on the boat with Tina."

"You sure you don't mind?"

"Your wife comes first," she said. "The baby too."

"Thanks, boss." His voice was shaky.

"Well, go on then," she told him. "Don't waste time on the phone with me. Look after that family of yours."

"Yes, boss." He hung up.

She stood back to survey the cottage, checking that no lights were on. There was no sign of movement. *Damn.*

PC McGuigan hadn't described the witness, and he would be leaving on the same boat with Johnny and Tina. Lesley would have to ask Ed to point the woman out for her.

She shook herself out, pulled her jacket tighter and hurried back towards the building where the staff meeting was being held.

CHAPTER TWENTY-FIVE

As Lesley approached the National Trust's admin building, her phone buzzed in her pocket. She fished it out, sighing. She just hoped it wasn't Johnny, saying he'd missed the boat.

It was a text from her daughter Sharon.

> I've had enough mum. I can't stand it anymore.

Lesley stopped walking. Why did teenagers insist on sending texts like that? The kind of message seemingly designed to create panic, and probably about nothing at all.

She couldn't leave it, though. She dialled Sharon's number and waited. It rang out three times and then clicked into voicemail.

"Sharon, it's Mum. I just got your text. Are you OK? Call me. Speak to you soon, love you."

She redialled Terry. Again, voicemail.

"Terry, it's Lesley. I've had a message from Sharon that's worried me a bit. She says she's had enough of something. Is she with you? Check on her, will you?"

She didn't like being hundreds of miles away, having to relay messages to Terry to keep an eye on their daughter.

Sharon and Terry had been arguing recently, or so Sharon had told her. Terry had refused to talk about the subject.

She straightened her jacket and pushed open the doors to the admin building. She could hear voices along the corridor and see light coming from a set of double doors. She took a moment to compose herself, standing where no one inside would be able to see her. She pulled on an air of professionalism and stepped through the doors.

Ed Rogers stood to one side, talking to a round-faced brunette next to him. She was tugging at her fingers, looking uneasy. Ed was doing his best to deflect questions. As he spotted Lesley, he beckoned her over.

"Everybody please," he said as she took her place next to him. "Let's all sit down and do this in an orderly manner. This is DCI Clarke, she's heading up the investigation into Simone's death."

Lesley gave the gathered staff a curt nod. She scanned the group for faces she recognised, but Johnny had done most of the interviews and she wasn't sure what Simone's team looked like. She wanted to watch them, observe their body language.

She put a hand on Ed's arm and turned away from the crowd, hoping he would do the same. He did. The brunette watched them, her eyes wide.

"Ed," she said to him. "Can I ask you a favour?"

"Of course you can."

"Natasha's team, identify them for me will you? In a way that's not obvious."

He nodded and turned back towards the room. He leaned his head towards Lesley as he spoke.

"Frankie Quinn, she's the one who found him. The black woman at the back, tall blonde man standing next to her, she's wearing a bright pink jacket."

"I see her," Lesley said.

"Then there's Anya Davinski, she's two rows in front of Frankie, thin blonde hair, wearing a National Trust fleece."

Lesley squinted. Half the room were wearing National Trust fleeces. Some of them were red, some green. A few of them had lanyards around their necks.

"Which one?" she asked him.

"The slim woman with bags under her eyes, chewing her fingernails."

"I see her."

Anya looked like it had been a few weeks since she'd had a square meal. She looked younger than her 44 years, and uncomfortable at being here. She'd been the last person to see Simone alive, so Lesley wasn't surprised she felt that way.

"And this is Natasha," Ed said, bringing his voice up so that the woman standing beside them could hear him. "Natasha Williams, Lesley Clarke. Lesley's the senior detective on this case. You don't mind me calling you Lesley, do you?"

"I don't."

Natasha gave her a nod. "Have you got anyone yet?" she asked. She had her hands in her pockets but Lesley could see she was fidgeting nonetheless.

"We don't have a suspect yet, but we are working on evidence that we hope will lead us to one."

Natasha took a shallow breath and looked away, into the crowd. Frankie Quinn, at the back, locked eyes with her. Lesley wondered which one was Diana Berry, the woman who'd overheard the argument.

She leaned in towards Ed. "I've got a potential witness," she muttered. "Diana Berry. Can you point her out to me?"

He squinted across the room then shook his head. "She's not here."

"No?"

"Uh-uh. She's got two young children, she'll be at home with them. Her husband's over there. Roger, large guy with thinning blonde hair, rainbow lanyard."

"I see him," Lesley said. "Does she normally not come to staff meetings?"

"They take it in turns," Ed said. "We've got a few couples on the island who work in much the same way. We don't have a lot of families, but we do have some who homeschool their kids or whose kids are below school age."

Lesley wondered why Diana hadn't answered the door, if she was at home. Ed cleared his throat and raised his hand to get people's attention.

"OK, everyone," he said. "Let's try and make this as brief as possible. I know you all want to get back home."

"We've been stuck in our homes all day," a man at the front said.

Ed turned to him. "Paul, I'm sure you understand why…"

"Yeah, yeah," the man, Paul, replied. "I just want to know when I'll able to do my job again."

"Tomorrow, I expect." Ed glanced at Lesley, who nodded. No point keeping them all locked up now the boats weren't running.

The man pursed his lips and muttered something indistinguishable.

Ed looked out at the assembled staff. Lesley counted twenty-seven people, most of them standing, some in chairs at the sides.

"I'm going to ask DCI Clarke to update you on where the investigation is," he said. "I'm sure you all want to know."

Lesley scanned the assembled staff. They'd gone quiet, waiting for news.

"Thank you for coming, everybody," she said. "As Ed told you, my name is DCI Clarke. I'm the senior investigating officer into Simone Browning's death."

There was a cough from the back.

"I'm sure word has got round that we examined Simone's body this morning and have determined that her death was suspicious. This means we're conducting a murder inquiry. I'm sure you'll all understand that means some changes to the way you work until we're able to conclude the investigation. Boats won't be allowed on or off the island without police authorisation, and there will be no visitors until the investigation is concluded."

Muttering ran through the room. "What about volunteers?" somebody called out.

Lesley shook her head. "Volunteers will be staying on the mainland for now. Only those of you already living here will be allowed to stay on the island."

"How do we get supplies?"

Lesley had expected them to be more worried about Simone's murder than about the logistics of being confined on the island.

"I'm sure Ed will help you manage that," she said. "We can authorise essential boat departures. But I imagine you're more concerned about the investigation into Simone's murder."

There was a sob from somewhere in the group. Lesley knew some SIOs liked to use euphemisms. But these people needed to know how one of their number had died. And that another of their number might well have killed her.

"I have to inform you," she said, "that our working theory is that somebody on this island killed Simone. We believe she was taken out in a boat and pushed into the harbour where she drowned. There's also evidence of a struggle between her and her attacker."

She paused, waiting for the words to sink in. Four people who had been standing sank into chairs. People's gazes shifted: away from Lesley and towards their colleagues. They were scared.

"I know our officers have spoken to many of you today. We need to know if you saw Simone in the last few days, or if you know anything that might help us identify her killer. We'll have uniformed officers and members of CID on the island over the next few days continuing with those interviews. Please, if you think of anything, no matter how small, tell us. Speak to Ed and we'll arrange an interview with you. Even if you've already spoken to one of my officers. If you have anything relevant to share, please tell us."

"Is there a phone number?" somebody asked.

It didn't seem worth setting up a hotline when the potential witnesses were all right here on this island, most of them in this room.

"Not right now," Lesley replied. "I'm sure you'll find it straightforward enough to get our attention if you need to speak to us. Like I say, whatever it is, no matter how inconsequential, if you saw or heard anything unusual over the last few days, or if you have any reason to suspect that somebody on this island or outside it might have wanted to hurt Simone… tell us, please."

More muttering.

Lesley turned to Ed. "I need to talk to you about the boat."

"Your crime scene manager has already updated me," he replied. "It's being impounded."

Lesley nodded. "I know it's inconvenient, but it's a potential crime scene."

He pursed his lips. "I'll have to ask John Lewis if they'll let us use their boat, until we can source another one. Hopefully regional office will help us out."

"Thanks."

Lesley turned back to the room. "We've established that Simone died between Monday evening and Tuesday morning. So if you saw or heard anything unusual during those times, please come forward. I'll be staying here on the island until the investigation is concluded and my colleagues will be here in the daytime."

More muttering. They wouldn't like the idea of a detective here full-time, but she knew it brought her closer to the case and to potential evidence.

Her phone buzzed. Sharon, Terry, or Johnny, she thought. Maybe Gail. She assumed Gail had gone back to the mainland with the uniformed constables, or she might still be working on that boat.

"OK, folks," said Ed.

Lesley's phone buzzed again.

Ed stepped forward to get the attention of the group. "If you have anything you want to tell the police, tell your line manager. They'll speak to me and I'll arrange for you to be interviewed. I'm in close contact with DCI Clarke, and we want to get this done as quickly as possible so we can get the island back to normal. Is everybody with me on that?"

There were murmurs of assent. Lesley's phone buzzed repeatedly in her pocket. Not a text, but a call.

"I have to take this," she muttered to Ed. She slipped out the room, aware that people were watching her.

She pulled out her phone: Terry. She felt her heart sink as she picked up.

"Did you get my message?" she asked.

"Yes," he said. "I'm worried sick. Do you know where she is?"

Lesley leaned against the wall. "What?"

"Sharon. She's disappeared."

Lesley pushed against the wall with her fingers, making her knuckles turn white. "Disappeared?"

"I came home from work today and she wasn't here," he said. "She's taken her rucksack."

Lesley swallowed. She could see tiny pinpricks in front of her eyes, like motes of dust. She hadn't eaten all day. She felt lightheaded.

"Have you called her?" she asked Terry.

"Of course I've bloody called her, I've been doing nothing else all night. That's why you couldn't get through to me. Where is she, Lesley?"

"How am I supposed to know?"

Ed's head came round the door. "Everything all right?" She nodded and waved him away.

"I need you to come home," Terry said. "We've got to find her."

Home. Lesley put her hand to the back of her neck, massaging the ache that was brewing. She'd been injured in a bomb attack eight months ago and stress brought the pain back.

"I can't just come back," she told him. "I'm on Brownsea Island. I'm staying here overnight."

"What? Where? Your daughter's more important, surely."

Lesley clenched her fist, drilling it into the wall. Even if she did go back to Birmingham, it would be hours.

"Find her, Terry. She's probably gone to a mate's house. Track her down and tell me when you've found her."

She hung up and left the building. It was almost dark, the island eerie in its quietness.

She didn't have Sharon's friends' phone numbers. But there were some mums whose numbers she'd saved when Sharon was younger. She started dialling, hoping this was a panic over nothing.

CHAPTER TWENTY-SIX

Frankie was approaching Natasha's house when she heard an unexpected sound.

She stopped walking and slowed her breathing. It was eight am and already the sun was warm, rising out to sea beyond the mouth of the harbour. She'd taken a stroll down to the quay, anxious to clear her head, and watched the light intensify, illuminating the Sandbanks peninsula as the mainland came to life.

Here by Natasha's house the air was still, the only sound the birds in the nearby trees. They were always more active in the morning, although the noise would have been twice as loud two hours ago.

But today there was another sound, a human sound. Somebody was crying.

Frankie approached the house and scanned the windows: nobody in sight. The sound intensified, interrupted by a sob.

She'd known Natasha for eighteen months, since she'd taken this job. Natasha's team was tight-knit, the four women depending on each other for company and support, both professional and personal.

But Simone had been closer to Natasha than Frankie was. Simone was one of those people it was impossible not to like. Fun when fun was called for, quiet and attentive when that was required. And bloody brilliant at her job.

Simone would have known exactly how to deal with Natasha crying.

But Simone wasn't here.

Frankie licked her lips, permanently dry and chapped from the sea air. She pulled in a breath and knocked on the door.

The crying stopped.

Frankie waited.

The crying started again.

She knocked for a second time.

"Natasha, it's Frankie. Are you OK?"

Silence.

Frankie stared at the door, wondering what she should do. If Natasha was crying in the privacy of her home, then maybe she would prefer to be left to it. And Bernard might be there to console her.

Simone would never have walked away.

Frankie cleared her throat and knocked. Firmly.

At last the door opened. Natasha stood in front of her, her face blotchy. She dragged the back of her hand across her cheek to wipe away tears.

"Frankie. Sorry, I didn't hear…"

"Are you OK?"

Natasha nodded. She sobbed, then wiped her nose with the sleeve of her hoody.

Frankie delved in her pocket and brought out a tissue. It was clean, if crumpled. She held it out and Natasha took it.

"Thanks." Natasha blew her nose. "You need something?"

"I just wanted to check you were OK. You seemed… distracted at the team meeting last night."

Natasha smiled. "I'm fine. It's all been a bit of a shock."

Frankie looked downwards. She felt insensitive, being in control of her emotions when Natasha was like this. Frankie had been fond of Simone too. It just hadn't sunk in yet.

"Is Bernard with you?"

A frown. "He got up early, went to the beach."

"The beach where…?"

Natasha nodded and sniffed. "The crime scene."

Frankie was horrified. If she never saw that beach again, it would be too soon. "Why?"

Natasha pulled in a shaky breath. "He's got a commission. One of the Nationals got wind of the fact that there's a journalist living on the island and…"

Frankie understood now. "Ah."

But still. How could you take work reporting on the death of a friend?

"He's over there now?" she asked.

"Yes." Frankie rubbed her nose with the corner of the tissue then stuffed it up her sleeve. "You need my help with something?"

"No. It's fine."

She had to get to work. They were allowed out of their houses now, safely marooned on the island with no boats running. She'd heard a rumour that the Trust's boat had been impounded by the police.

Frankie reached out and touched Natasha's arm. "Call me if you need me, OK?"

"I'll be fine. It's a lot to deal with."

Frankie nodded. She turned away and made for the woods in the centre of the island, wishing she could shake this numbness.

CHAPTER TWENTY-SEVEN

Lesley woke to find the sun streaming through the thin curtains of the cottage she'd been allocated. It was a squat, narrow building, looking out over the water towards Poole. It had the shadow of damp running up the walls and a sense of neglect. She wondered who normally used it, if anyone.

She grabbed her phone and checked messages and voicemail. Nothing. She raised her phone, standing up on the bed. No signal.

Damn. *Sharon, where are you?*

She could only hope Terry had found her. Her daughter was Terry's responsibility when she was in Birmingham, and she was sixteen. But that didn't stop her worrying.

She jumped to the wooden floor, wishing she'd been able to get a change of clothes brought over. She'd slept in her underwear, and yesterday's shirt hung over a chair in the corner, along with her suit. She picked it up, flapped it out to get some air into it and considered putting it on. *No*, she told herself, *have a wash first*.

She'd grabbed Diana Berry's husband at the end of the staff meeting and asked if she could speak to his wife. But he'd insisted that Diana would be fast asleep by now. Apparently she was in the habit of hitting the sack the moment her youngest child fell asleep. Lesley's first job today would be to go and find the woman.

She walked into the pokey bathroom, relieved to find soap on the sink, and washed herself. She returned to the bedroom, flapping her arms to dry herself off and wishing she had something to use as a towel. She cracked the curtains open and peered through. Sunlight glinted off the harbour. It would have been idyllic if only the house was nicer.

She pulled her hands through her hair, peering into a small mirror over a chest of drawers that looked like it would collapse if she touched it. Next came her shirt. It smelt sweaty. She'd wear her jacket to cover it up, heat be damned.

Lesley liked to present herself well. Her smart suits and crisp blouses might not be the latest fashion, but they made her look professional and trustworthy. If she smelt like a tramp, people wouldn't open up to her.

She shrugged on her jacket and clattered down the stairs. There was no point going into the kitchen, there were no supplies. She hoped she could get something in the café.

On the doorstep, she could see the quay. Gail had been here till eleven o'clock last night, examining every inch of that boat before it had been lifted onto a haulage boat and transported over to Poole. Gail and her colleague Gavin had gone with it, leaving Lesley the only member of the investigating team on the island. She could only hope Johnny would be back soon with Tina and her colleagues. They needed to get a crack on with these interviews.

She yawned, tugged at the skin under her eyes and turned towards the castle and the admin building in its shadow.

As she neared the castle, her phone picked up a signal and pinged. A text from Elsa, sent at 10pm last night.

> Sharon's at my flat. Call me.

Lesley stopped in her tracks. She read the text again. She checked the sender. It was Elsa all right, not Terry.

Sharon had come all the way to Bournemouth and turned up at Elsa's flat. Did that mean she'd gone to Lesley's house in Wareham first, or had she gone straight to the flat knowing it was closer to the station?

Sharon knew that Lesley spent most weeknights at Elsa's flat. Even so, the thought of her sixteen-year-old daughter landing in Bournemouth and knocking on doors in the hope of finding her filled Lesley with guilt.

She dialled Elsa. Voicemail. Why was nobody picking up?

"Elsa, it's me. I just got your text. I'm stuck on Brownsea Island on a case and didn't have a signal last night, sorry. Is Sharon still with you? Call me or get her to call me."

She hung up and dialled Sharon's number: no answer. Sharon never answered her phone. She sent her a text.

> Elsa tells me you're at hers. Call me, let me know you're OK. Mum x.

She hesitated then deleted the *x*. She pulled in a breath and rang Terry.

"What is it?" he snapped. "Tell me you've found her."

"Hey," she said. "Don't take it out on me."

"You won't believe the night I've had," he replied. "I've been driving around Edgbaston and Harborne, knocking on the doors of her friends."

"Don't you have their phone numbers?"

"What do you think?"

"Anyway," she replied. "She's turned up, she's in Bournemouth."

"Bournemouth?" he repeated.

"Yes." Lesley bit her fingernail. Terry didn't know about Elsa. "One of my friends," she said. "Sharon turned up at her flat, she thought I might be there."

"But you're on Brownsea Island."

"Sharon didn't know that."

"I looked it up," he told her. "What the hell are you doing there?"

"Check the news. There's been a murder here."

"Another one? You're not very good for the death rate, are you?"

Lesley didn't reply to that.

"I'll call you when I speak to her," she said. "I'll tell her she needs to go home."

"You haven't spoken to her yet? What the hell—"

She hung up, then regretted it. She hadn't asked him what had happened to make Sharon leave Birmingham without telling him. To provoke that *I've had enough* text. She could guess, though. Terry's girlfriend Julieta, and her son.

Lesley redialled to find his number engaged. She wasn't about to leave a message.

She was past the farm buildings now, halfway to Diana Berry's house. She needed to click into professional mode. Stop being a mum and start being a copper. But she still didn't know where Sharon was. Was she at Elsa's, or had she set off for Wareham?

Lesley pulled a hand through her hair. She texted her daughter again.

> Stay at Elsa's. Call me, tell me you're safe.

It was all she could do. Sharon was sixteen. Legally she could take care of herself. But in real life, it didn't work like that.

Diana Berry's house was up ahead. Lesley squared her shoulders, pulled her jacket straight, and sniffed at the air, checking the faint scent of her own armpits. She knocked on the door, hoping the witness wouldn't notice.

CHAPTER TWENTY-EIGHT

Elsa Short parked her car around the corner from the beach and closed the door. She looked up and down the coast road, shuddering as she caught a glimpse of the apartment building in which she'd been imprisoned a month earlier. Priscilla Evans, the girlfriend of her old business partner Harry Nevin, had locked her in overnight. If Lesley hadn't turned up in time, she had no doubt the woman would have killed her.

She shook the tension out of her body. *Get a grip*. She needed to be sharp for this meeting. She turned the corner and approached the café in the side road leading to the beach. She'd been in the habit of meeting Harry here on alternate Wednesday mornings. A regular occurrence, to discuss cases they preferred not to talk about in the office. Until Harry had been murdered by his insane girlfriend.

She took a table outside the café and scanned the area. There was no sign of the woman she was meeting. Elsa hadn't been expecting to return here after Harry's death. But a text had arrived this morning: *We need to talk, same place you used to meet Harry.*

Elsa had left Sharon in her flat, sulking on the sofa about something her dad had done. Elsa loved Lesley, but she wasn't keen on becoming a surrogate mother to her daughter.

A waitress appeared and Elsa ordered a double espresso. She needed the caffeine shot, she'd been up late trying to convince Sharon to call her dad. But Sharon had been insistent: she'd had enough of her dad. She hated his new girlfriend's little boy and she wanted to come down here to Bournemouth for good.

Elsa hadn't bargained on becoming a stepmum when she'd met Lesley and she wasn't sure how she felt about it. If only Lesley had picked up her phone.

"Good morning, Elsa."

Elsa turned to see a woman standing behind her. Early sixties, with greying hair piled on top of her head. She wore an expensive lime-green suit and heels that were too high for a café by the beach.

Elsa gave the woman a nod. "Morning, Aurelia."

Aurelia Cross sat down. She was the third member of their legal partnership, the Cross in Nevin, Cross and Short. They still hadn't changed the name of the firm.

Harry had been the founding partner; it seemed disrespectful to take his name off the door. But Elsa knew that at some point, they would need to replace him. Whether they'd recruit internally from the junior partners or they'd look outside the firm, she wasn't sure. She imagined Aurelia had a view on it. Aurelia tended to have a view on everything.

The waitress reappeared with Elsa's coffee and took Aurelia's order for a pot of herbal tea. Aurelia placed her bag on the seat next to her as the waitress walked away. It was expensive, designer.

"So," she said, leaning back in her chair and eyeing Elsa. "You used to meet Harry here on a regular basis."

Elsa met her gaze. "I did."

"And I don't suppose I need to ask what you met to discuss."

"I don't suppose you do."

Aurelia had never got involved with the firm's biggest client. Elsa had been assigned to his account not long after joining the firm, Harry handing the reins over to her eagerly. But Aurelia had refused to go near the man.

"Are things going as they should?" Aurelia asked.

Elsa shrugged. "Difficult to say what 'as they should' is when it comes to this particular client."

"No recent arrests among his people? No nosing around by the police?"

Elsa shook her head. "Nothing."

"All financial affairs above board?"

Elsa locked eyes with her partner and returned the woman's smile. They both knew Elsa wasn't about to give a truthful answer to that question.

The client in question, Arthur Kelvin, kept accounts that looked regular enough, on the surface. He paid his accountant a lot of money to make it so. But the accountant and Elsa both knew that the figures submitted to the authorities each year hid a multitude of sins. Kelvin had a wide variety of constantly changing businesses, new concerns being added and subtracted from his portfolio on an almost weekly basis. Some were above board. Others were designed as a smokescreen for his real activities. Elsa had some knowledge of which was which, but wasn't allowed the full facts.

"Everything's under control," she told Aurelia. "You don't need to worry."

"So the investigation into Harry's death didn't cause the police to look at your client list?"

"Why would it?"

"I thought you got Ameena Khan involved in a couple of cases?"

Elsa swallowed. Ameena Khan had been a junior partner, she'd died two days before Harry. And she'd been sleeping with him, it turned out. Along with Priscilla Evans, the woman who'd killed him.

"Ameena was only tangentially involved," she said. "Once the police found out Harry and Ameena had been having an affair, they realised there wasn't any point digging into his clients. You don't need to worry, Aurelia."

"Good."

Aurelia stopped talking as the waitress reappeared. She placed a tray on the table and offloaded a pot of tea and a cup. Aurelia nodded her thanks and poured for herself.

"Is that all you wanted to speak to me about?" Elsa asked.

Aurelia took a sip from her tea and grimaced: *hot*. "I just want to make sure you keep all this separate from the firm's other undertakings."

"Of course," Elsa replied. "That's what I've always done."

Elsa had been hoping that Harry's death would mean the breakup of the firm. At the very least she'd hoped it would scare Arthur Kelvin away. She wanted out.

If Kelvin ever got caught, she would be too.

And now she was shacked up with a copper. Was she stupid? Or was she just naive?

CHAPTER TWENTY-NINE

Diana Berry sat at the kitchen table in her cottage, her fingers entwined around a mug of coffee. Lesley sat opposite her, having refused the offer of a cup. Between them, at the end of the table, sat a small girl, three or four years old. She was colouring in a picture of children at the seaside. Lesley wondered if the girl had made the connection between her own life and the imagined one in the picture.

Diana's eyes were clouded. She yawned and took a long gulp of her coffee.

"My colleague PC McGuigan has told me you witnessed something on Monday night," Lesley said to her.

Diana nodded, then glanced at the little girl. "Two women," she said, "arguing."

Lesley looked her in the eye. "Did you *see* anything?"

"Nothing. I was over by the quay taking a walk. I sometimes go out at night when the kids are in bed and my husband's catching up on his work. It's calm at that time, peaceful. It allows me to think."

Lesley nodded. "What time was this?"

The woman frowned, thinking. "I reckon it was about nine o'clock." A pause. "Yeah. I left the house at quarter to, I remember checking the clock before I told Simon where I was going. So by the time I got to the quay, and had stood there for a while… I like to look out to sea," she said, looking embarrassed. "Collecting my thoughts."

"And you heard two women?" Lesley asked her.

Diana reached out and touched her daughter on the hand. "Charlie love. Why don't you go upstairs and get your Play-doh down?"

The girl frowned. "I like this."

"Please, love. Just fetch it down and we can make stuff together."

The girl looked at her mum for a moment, then shrugged and climbed down from her chair. Diana watched as she left the room, closing the door behind her. Lesley heard the thump of feet running up the stairs and turned back to the girl's mother.

"Tell me what you heard."

"I heard a woman shouting, first. Screaming blue murder she was."

"Could you make out any words?"

"Not much. It was a way away."

"So where was she?"

"Over towards the church. The woman was… well, she wasn't happy."

"And you didn't catch any words at all?"

"Oh, I caught some. Ripe they were, the woman had a mouth like a toilet bowl."

Lesley smiled. She'd talked like that before she'd met Dennis and had been forced to tone down her language.

"And then you heard another woman?" she asked.

Diana nodded. She took another slurp of her coffee and leaned back in her chair. "The second woman's voice was lower, quieter, but it was definitely a woman. She was trying to calm the first woman down, but the first woman just kept yelling at her."

"Did you approach them?" Lesley asked her.

"I walked up towards the church. I stood by the wall to the castle. There were two figures, they were at the side of the church on the path leading up to the hides."

"Did you see their faces?"

Diana shook her head. "Sorry. They disappeared not long after I got there."

"Which way did they go?" Lesley asked. "Did they both go the same way?"

"I saw one of them heading over towards the farm buildings, and then when I looked back at the church, the other one was gone. I'm not sure where she went, but I assume…"

"You assume what?"

"Well, I assume she went up to the houses past the hides." She looked at Lesley. "There's only two women who live up there, Simone Browning and Frankie Quinn."

Lesley nodded slowly. "Those are the only houses on that side of the island?"

"There's a visitor centre up there, a small one. It covers the habitats on that side of the island, and then there's the two houses. Frankie and Adam live in one, Simone lived in the other."

"So you think one of the women was either Simone or Frankie?"

A shrug. "I can't be sure, all I can say is which way she went."

"And the other woman went up towards the farm buildings?"

"Yes."

And the beach, Lesley thought. The beach where Simone had been found.

"OK." She fished her card out of the inside pocket of her jacket. "If you think of anything else, call me." She jabbed at the card. "This is my mobile number. I'm staying on the island, so you can call me day or night."

Diana pocketed the card. "I will."

The door opened and the little girl clattered in, hauling a plastic box. "Are we going to play now, Mum?"

Diana looked at Lesley. "Are we done here?"

"I think so," Lesley told her.

"Good." She turned to her daughter. "Come on then Charlie, let's see what we can make."

CHAPTER THIRTY

Dr Whittaker was playing classical music for the post-mortem. Wagner's *Flying Dutchman* this time, a sea-inspired tune. Dennis found it disconcerting, the sudden crescendos taking him by surprise in the incongruous surroundings.

He stood a few paces back and watched as the pathologist examined Simone's body. He worked his way over her flesh, looking for bruises and other marks. Whittaker paused at Simone's neck, moving her head from side to side to get a better angle. He stood back and let his assistant take photographs as he progressed.

"Those finger-marks," Dennis said, "Strangulation, you think?"

Whittaker glanced up at him. "Let me finish, man."

Dennis bristled. Whittaker could be tetchy, but the two men had known each other for decades and he normally treated Dennis with a modicum of respect.

Whittaker walked around the table and examined the other side of the neck. He sniffed and stood up straight, looking at Dennis.

"I can answer your question now."

Dennis raised an eyebrow. "And?"

"Somebody *tried* to strangle her. There are clear finger imprints, two at the front, five at the back."

"But that's not how she died?"

Whittaker took a pencil out of the top pocket of his lab coat and used it to hold the woman's mouth slightly open. "There was foaming here. Most of it's gone now, but there was plenty when we picked her up on the beach. Unmistakeable sign that her lungs filled with water."

Dennis knew about the signs of drowning. You couldn't work in a county like Dorset and not see a few drownings in your time.

"So that's what killed her?"

Whittaker nodded. "Maybe she was unconscious when she went in, the strangulation might have made her black out. Her assailant might have thought she was dead and he pushed her in to remove the evidence."

"He?" Dennis asked.

Whittaker shook his head. "You know what I mean, man."

"I don't. Are you telling me you think this was a man?"

"Whoever it was, male or female, they were strong enough to get her onto a boat and then push her into the harbour."

"Or clever enough to convince her to get on the boat," Dennis said.

The pathologist shrugged. "Most killers are men, especially most strangulation killers."

Dennis knew he was right. Women were more likely to use an indirect method for murder. Poison, sleeping tablets. With men, it was more common for the victim to have physical marks. When contact was made with the victim, a woman was more likely to take a knife than she was to put her hand on her victim's body.

"Any defensive wounds?" Dennis asked the pathologist.

"Not that I can see. There are some nibble marks on her toes where the fish got her, and the skin on her fingers is peeling away a little. Not what I'd class as gloving, she wasn't in the water for long enough, but some evidence of damage."

"So if she did have any evidence on her hands, we wouldn't be able to see it?"

"Afraid not." Whittaker stood back and surveyed the body, his fingers brushing his chin. He'd grown a moustache since Dennis had worked with him last.

"So you still think she was in the water for about twenty-four hours?" Dennis asked.

"It could have been less, I'd say anything from eighteen to twenty-four based on what I can see here."

That was a wider window. Dennis wondered how Lesley was getting on, whether she'd found people who'd seen Simone during that time.

"Right," said Whittaker. "Time to open her up. I'm pretty sure we'll get confirmation that she drowned. Do you want to hang around to see?"

Dennis looked at the body. He needed to get back to the office. He'd had a call from Johnny last night saying he was returning from the island. Dennis wanted to make sure everything was alright with the constable, and he also needed to brief Lesley.

"It's fine," he said. "Send me your report when you've got it."

Whittaker looked impatient. "Of course I will."

CHAPTER THIRTY-ONE

Lesley turned in her chair as Gail and Tina entered the office they'd been allocated by the National Trust.

"Morning," she said. "Decent journey over?"

Gail grimaced. "A bit choppy today."

Lesley looked out of the window. It had been sunny when she'd arrived, but now there were clouds over the harbour and she could see that the water was uneven. Johnny was probably still on the quay, trying not to chuck up.

"How's progress with the boat?" she asked Gail.

"It's in dry storage over in Poole," the CSM replied. "We've analysed the seat, top and bottom. All we've got is that one patch of blood. I've sent samples away for DNA analysis. I'll be back at the beach today, giving it the final once-over."

"Good," said Lesley. "When can we expect the DNA results back?"

"A few days."

Lesley frowned. She didn't like waiting.

"Did you find anything elsewhere on the boat? Hairs? Fibres? I don't suppose we'd be so lucky as to have had the killer drop their shoe or something?"

Gail grimaced. "I'm afraid we're all out of stupid killers this week."

Lesley leaned back in her chair. She craned her neck to look up at the ceiling. Her back ached; the bed in the cottage was too soft.

"Ah, stupid killers," she said. "I wish we had more of those."

Lesley caught movement out of the corner of her eye and sat up. The three PCs entered the room, gathering around Tina. Another uniformed officer was behind them, a sergeant.

Lesley gave him a nod. "Sergeant."

"Ma'am," he replied. "I'm Sergeant Dillick. I'm here to coordinate our officers today."

Lesley glanced at Tina. As far as she was aware, Tina had been doing a good job of it. But Uniform wouldn't like a PC who'd been drafted into CID bossing their guys around.

"Of course," she said.

Regardless of the politics, an extra officer would mean more interviews. Hopefully they would be able to speak to everybody today.

"Is DC Chiles with you?" she asked.

Dillick frowned. "No one else, Ma'am."

Lesley looked at Gail. She'd been expecting Johnny back.

She made a note to check with Dennis. He'd probably spoken to the DC. She hoped Johnny's wife was OK.

"I want to prioritise the John Lewis people," she said.

"You sure?" replied Gail. "Surely the National Trust people were closer to Simone, more likely to have a motive."

Lesley shook her head. "Yolanda Harte wants to get them all out of here on a boat later today. I want us to find out if they saw anything before they disappear."

The sergeant nodded. "I'll get on to it, Ma'am," he said. "We've got the list."

The sergeant left the room, taking his three officers with him. Tina was about to leave when Lesley raised a hand to stop her.

"Hang on a minute, Tina. You wait here while we have the briefing."

"Briefing, boss?" Tina asked.

"I'm calling in to Dennis. Get the office on speak-erphone, will you."

"Of course."

Tina lowered herself into a chair and pulled out her mobile phone. She dialled and put the phone on the table.

After a few moments, Dennis's voice came over the speaker.

"Morning all," he said.

Tina pushed her phone into the centre of the table.

"You're ready for us?" Lesley asked.

"More than," Dennis replied. "I've just come from the post-mortem."

Lesley checked her watch: half past nine. "Whittaker *is* getting up early these days."

"Don't knock it."

She smiled. "Anything new from the PM?"

"Nothing," he replied. "We've got attempted strangulation marks on her neck but Whittaker is confident it was drowning that killed her."

"So she wasn't strangled, and then pushed in?"

"If she was, the strangling wasn't enough to finish her off. Might have made her easier to push in, but it was the water that killed her. There's foaming around her mouth. I'm expecting confirmation that her lungs will show signs of having been full of water."

"OK," she said. "So her killer tried to strangle her and then pushed her in the water. The question is, did he think she was dead already, or did he do that to finish the job?"

"And what about that blood?" asked Gail.

"That'll all depend on whose it is," Lesley said. "It might be unrelated."

"I doubt it," Gail replied. "Hell of a coincidence."

Lesley sighed. She didn't want to rely on a piece of evidence that she couldn't expect to know more about for a few days.

"We'll work with what we've got for now," she said. "We need to know who took that boat out. I've got a witness who heard two women arguing late on Monday night. One of them could have been Simone, but we're not sure. We need to know if anyone else saw anything and if that boat was seen going out Monday night, or early Tuesday morning."

"Are we sure that Anya's story is correct?" Dennis asked. "Meeting Simone for a drink?"

"Might be, might not," Lesley said. "You think it was Anya having the argument with Simone?"

"It's a possibility. Perhaps Anya killed her."

"It's too much of a leap based on what we've got," Lesley said. "We need to find out who this argument was between, whether Simone was one of the participants, and if so, whether it's related to her death."

"Do you want me to speak to the conservation team?" Tina asked.

Lesley nodded. "Yes. Anya first, then Natasha, followed by Frankie. Run through their stories again, check for inconsistencies. And with Anya in particular, I want the specifics of what she and Simone did on Monday night.

What time they met, where they went, what they talked about. Get details, check out her story."

"Should I ask if she had an argument with her?"

"Yes," Lesley replied. "No point beating about the bush."

"And then there's Bernard Williams," Mike said over the speaker.

"What about him?" Lesley asked.

"He was the one Simone spoke to when she called in sick. Who's to say he's telling the truth?"

"Do you think he's lying? Covering for somebody?"

"Covering for his wife maybe?" said Dennis.

Lesley looked out of the window towards the sea. "See if you can find him as well," she told Tina. "Get him separately from his wife, check their movements on Monday and Tuesday. Again, I'm looking for inconsistencies."

"Yes, boss."

Tina stood up, about to leave the room, then remembered that her mobile phone was being used as a speakerphone. She looked at it and sat down.

"Is Johnny with you?" Lesley asked Dennis.

"Not yet. I thought he'd be back on the island."

"He wasn't on the boat."

"I'll speak to him. I assume he's with his wife."

Lesley looked at Tina. "How was he on the boat last night?"

"Green around the gills," Tina replied. "Stressed. He was sweating, looked like he was going to throw up."

"That's Johnny and boats," Lesley said. "Give him a call, Dennis. I don't want him to feel that we've abandoned him."

"That was my plan after this conversation, boss."

"Of course." Lesley realised that Tina was still with them. "Tina, did you get that bag for me? Overnight stuff?"

"I didn't have time to go to your house, so I went to Marks and Spencers in Bournemouth. I hope that's OK? I figured…"

Lesley knew what the younger woman was thinking. She wasn't known for her fashion sense, but at least she was presentable. Marks and Spencers was cheaper than her usual clothes, a bit shabbier, but it would work.

A plastic carrier bag leaned against the wall by the door. Tina put it on the desk. Lesley removed it, placing it on the floor by her feet. She would worry about that later.

"OK," she said. "Tina, let's get out there and start those interviews. Gail, tell me if you find anything else on the boat or the beach. Dennis, give Johnny my best will you?"

"No problem, boss."

CHAPTER THIRTY-TWO

Lesley hurried out of the café building, heading towards the castle. She needed to find Yolanda Harte before those boats arrived and took her staff off the island.

She stopped at the gates, glad she knew where the intercom was this time, and leaned on the buzzer.

After a moment the gate opened. The same woman who'd answered it yesterday, Greta, stood looking at her.

"Can I help you?" she asked, looking for all the world like she had no idea who Lesley was.

"I need to speak to Yolanda Harte."

"She's in a conference call with head office."

"I'll wait."

Lesley stepped through the gate, determined not to let the woman shut her out.

"I'll sit out here," she said, nodding towards a bench facing out towards the harbour.

Greta shrugged. "I'll tell her you're here."

Lesley made for the bench and threw herself down.

She felt restless and irritable. She didn't like not knowing what was behind the tension between the two groups of residents. She didn't like not knowing who was telling the truth about Simone Browning's movements before she died. And she didn't like being stuck on this island while Sharon was gallivanting around the country.

She took out her phone and dialled Elsa, who picked up on the second ring.

Lesley slumped back in the bench, relieved to have got through.

"Hey El," she said.

"Hello, sweetie. D'you want to know how Sharon is?"

"I'm so sorry she turned up at yours like that."

"It's fine." Elsa's voice was terse. "She's still at the flat, I'm at work."

"Of course." Lesley couldn't possibly expect her girlfriend to stay home and look after her daughter. "How long is she planning on staying?"

"She didn't say, she wants to wait until you get back."

Damn.

"I don't know how long I'll be stuck over here."

She would have to find a boat, go back to see Sharon and then return to the island to continue the investigation. She didn't like being derailed like this. But she was a single mum now, and she knew that was all about juggling responsibilities. She'd seen it often enough with her colleagues. She'd seen it at close hand with Zoe Finch.

"OK," she said. "There'll be a boat leaving here this afternoon, I'll come back."

And then she'd have to return tomorrow morning with Tina and the other PCs, if they needed to return.

"Again, I'm really sorry Els. I didn't expect her to turn up on your door."

Elsa grunted. "She's not happy, you know."

"What about?"

"Her and Terry. I don't know what's going on between them, but she's pissed off."

"She doesn't like his new girlfriend's son," Lesley said. "He's just a kid. Getting in her way I suppose."

Things were tough for Sharon right now. One parent at the opposite end of the country, busy with work as ever. And the other building himself a new family. Sharon had been desperate enough to book herself a train ticket, find her way to Dorset without telling anybody, and turn up not just at Lesley's door, but Elsa's.

"Did she go to mine first?" she asked Elsa, "Before she came to you?"

"Apparently yes. She got a taxi. She's nicked Terry's credit card. Knew his PIN."

Lesley grinned. "Resourceful of her."

"She keeps saying he's going to kill her for it."

"He'll be fine," Lesley replied.

The least he could do was pay for his daughter's escape, if he was the one who'd brought it about.

Lesley spotted Yolanda Harte walking down a broad flight of steps. Her lips were pursed and her body language tight.

"I have to go," she said. "I'll call you, let you know when I'm getting back."

And she'd speak to Sharon too.

"OK, speak to you later. Love you." Elsa hung up.

Lesley held the phone out in front of her, her chest light. Elsa hadn't said that to her before.

She put her phone in her pocket, struggling to switch to DCI mode, and looked up at Yolanda. The woman was standing between Lesley and the sun, forcing Lesley to squint to see her.

"You were looking for me?" Yolanda asked.

"I want to speak to your staff before they get on a boat. I'm sure you understand that it's important that we—"

Yolanda waved a hand in dismissal. "I understand, Detective, and I've arranged a staff meeting for ten o'clock this morning. You can address them all there. Does that work for you?"

"That works perfectly, thank you."

Lesley had no idea if there were any individuals among the John Lewis staff who could be of help. That being the case, the easiest thing was to get them all in one room and ask them to come forward if they'd seen anything. Yolanda had done the right thing.

She stood up and brushed down her skirt. She'd left that Marks and Spencers bag back in the office, but she needed to find time to go back to the cottage and get changed. She was still in yesterday's underwear. She felt rank and sticky.

"I'll see you at ten o'clock," she told Yolanda. In the meantime, Tina would need her help with those interviews.

CHAPTER THIRTY-THREE

Anya Davinski was a slim blonde woman with thin, straggly hair. She opened the door to Tina and her face fell at the sight of the uniform.

"Oh," she said. "You need me again?"

Tina gave her a tight smile. "Sorry to bother you, Ms Davinski. Do you mind if I come in?"

The woman shrugged. She stood back to let Tina in, not looking happy about it.

Tina walked through to a low-ceilinged sitting room. She looked back at Anya, who gestured towards an armchair. Tina took it, placing her hands in her lap. She took her notepad out. Anything to keep her hands busy, to alleviate the tension.

Anya took the matching armchair opposite, leaving the sofa between them empty. The room was so cramped it was barely possible to move around it. Tina wondered if whoever had chosen the furniture had ever seen the room.

"Thanks for talking to me again," she said. "I wanted to ask you a few more questions about when you saw Simone on Monday night."

Anya gave her a slow nod. "I thought you would be back."

"Why's that?"

The woman shrugged. "I was the last person to see her alive, I suppose you might think I did it."

Tina frowned. "Why might you think that?"

"The last person to see her alive, the first person to suspect. I didn't, though. Simone was alive when she left me."

"Can you remind me what the two of you did when you met up?"

"We sat outside the café, we use the tables there when it's closed. She brought two tins of lager. There is no pub here. Sitting there, it feels more like going out than sitting in someone's house."

Tina had been trying to imagine what it would be like to live here, a population of just forty-two and nothing to occupy you after finishing work for the day. These people must be consumed by their work.

"How did Simone seem when she left you?" she asked.

A shrug. "Fine, normal."

"Did she leave you at the café or did you walk back towards her house with her?"

"I already told your colleague. The thin man."

"Please. We're just checking."

Anya gave her a look. "Why do you ask?"

"Just wondering."

"She left me at the café, I was sitting on the bench when she left."

"And what time was this?"

"Nine o'clock, something like that? We weren't looking at the time."

"But you had to be up early the next morning for work."

"My house is a five minute walk from my work," Anya told her. "One minute from the café. It's not like I have a commute."

"No. So did the two of you fall out while you were talking?"

"Fall out?"

"Did you argue?"

"No."

"What did you talk about?"

"She was telling me about a new project she's working on. A squirrel thing, for Natasha."

"And did you talk about what you were working on?"

Anya shook her head. "I talked about my boyfriend. Pavel, he lives in Poland. I think he has found another woman."

"So the two of you were on good terms when she left you?"

"We were. I was sad. I didn't know what to do about Pavel. Simone tried to make me feel better."

"Was she going straight home?" Tina asked.

"I didn't ask, why would I? There's nowhere else to go."

"And how long did you stay outside the café after she left you?"

"Two minutes. No more than five. I looked at the lights coming on over the harbour, thinking about home. I lived on the coast, a place called Leba. Lots of wildlife, not many people. This island is like that too, especially in the winter."

"And did you hear anything after Simone left you?"

"Anything like what?"

"Did you hear her talking to anyone else? An argument maybe?"

"You already asked if I had an argument with her. No."

"Not necessarily with you," Tina replied. "But could you have heard an argument between her and someone else?"

"I heard nothing. I stared out to sea, I stood up, I went home, I went to bed. I got up in the morning and went to work. Next time I heard about Simone was when she did not arrive at the team meeting."

"Were you puzzled by that, given that you'd seen her the previous night?"

"I assumed she had a hangover."

"So she drank a lot?"

"No, but Simone was not good with alcohol."

Tina nodded. To call in sick when you lived minutes away from your work seemed unusual if Simone had a hangover induced by a couple of beers. Could she have suddenly fallen ill? Or had that argument kept her from coming into work?

The other possibility was that she was already dead. In which case, she hadn't called in sick at all.

CHAPTER THIRTY-FOUR

As Lesley returned to the quay, she spotted Tina leaving a cottage over towards the lagoon. Lesley gave her a wave to summon her over.

"Whose house was that?"

"Anya Davinski. She says she met Simone for a drink on Monday night and that they didn't argue."

"Nothing at all? They didn't fall out over anything?"

Tina shook her head. "She said they had a friendly evening and then Simone left her. Anya went home, Simone headed off to her cottage. Anya didn't hear anything."

Lesley dragged her hand through her hair and looked out to sea. "So the next person she spoke to is Bernard Williams. I'll go and talk to him and his wife."

"You want me to speak to Frankie Quinn?" Tina asked.

"Yes," Lesley replied. "I'm not expecting much more from her, but it can't do any harm to cover the whole team. I've got a meeting in the castle to go to before the John Lewis people leave the island and then I'm just hoping we get something more from Gail."

She slumped onto a bench looking out over the harbour, tiredness washing over her. "We're getting nowhere. One of these people is hiding something.

Somebody fell out with Simone, and that somebody could have been the person that killed her."

"Or could have seen the person who killed her maybe?" Tina suggested.

Lesley shrugged. "You talk to Frankie, I'll talk to Natasha and Bernard. Let me know if you find anything useful."

"No problem, boss."

Frankie Quinn lived with her partner Adam in the house next door to the one Simone had occupied. It was a fifteen minute walk from the quayside. Lesley watched Tina walking briskly away, and then turned and began to trudge in the other direction, towards the Williams's house, dragging her heels. As she passed the church she heard the familiar shriek of the peacock. She turned and peered into the churchyard. Sure enough it was wandering around, looking bored.

"What did you see on Monday night?" she muttered to the creature.

She shook herself out and carried on walking. Twenty minutes later she was knocking on the Williams's front door.

Natasha opened it almost immediately. Her eyes were red-rimmed and her hair hadn't been washed.

"Come in," she said, her voice flat.

Lesley followed her through into the kitchen. The lights were out and the room was dark. Behind here were the woods where the squirrels reputedly lived. It meant very little sun got into this kitchen. The room was gloomy, the woman standing opposite her gloomier still.

Lesley stood next to the table, placing a hand on its surface. "I want to ask you if you knew anything about Simone falling out with someone."

Natasha frowned. "Who?"

Lesley looked into her eyes. "A woman. We don't know who."

Natasha leaned against the sink, her body slack. "Simone never fell out with anyone. She was one of those people who everybody liked. She was kind, funny." She looked down at the floor. "I have no idea who would want to kill her."

Lesley watched Natasha carefully. Her movements were steady even if they did indicate a woman who was deeply distressed. She didn't appear to be lying.

"She rang you early on Tuesday morning," Lesley said, "Called in sick."

Natasha looked and nodded. "She spoke to Bernard, my husband."

"Is he here?"

"He's over at…" Natasha tailed off.

"Where is he?" Lesley asked. "I'll need to speak to him."

Natasha swallowed, her cheeks flushed. "He's probably at the beach where we found her."

"Why would he be there?"

Natasha pushed her shoulders back, trying to project confidence. "He's a journalist. He's reporting on the crime."

Lesley felt her nostrils flare. So Bernard Williams was profiting from Simone's death. The press had their job to do, she supposed. Maybe she could speak with him, make sure that what he published would help them find the killer.

"OK," she said. "I'll go and find him. But can you tell me what reason she gave for calling in sick?"

"Some sort of bug, Bernard told me. She had sickness and diarrhoea."

Tina hadn't mentioned Anya saying anything about a bug. The two women had been sitting in the garden outside the café, drinking.

"It wasn't a hangover?" Lesley asked.

"Oh, no," Natasha replied. "Simone would never get drunk on a work night."

"Anya says the two of them met up on Monday night, that they went for a drink in the garden of the café."

Natasha nodded. "They did that regularly. I joined them sometimes, Frankie too. It's different for us because we've got partners, but Simone and Anya were close."

"And how would you say their relationship was?" Lesley asked her.

"Good. Like I say, Simone got along with everybody. She was that sort of woman."

It was the second time Natasha had said this. Lesley wondered if Natasha resented Simone being the kind of person everyone liked. Lesley had managed people like that. It wasn't always easy to avoid feeling threatened by them.

"And how was *your* relationship with Simone?" she asked.

"Excellent," Natasha said. "She was a high performing member of the team."

"What about your personal relationship. Were you friends?"

"All four of us are friends," Natasha said. "Were. You become close to your colleagues when you live here."

Lesley nodded. "Had she suffered from stomach bugs before? Did she call in sick frequently?"

"Never." Natasha gripped the edge of the sink. "It was the first time she'd called in sick since she started working here."

Lesley pulled in a breath. "And you didn't think to tell me that before?"

Simone had been killed on Monday night or Tuesday morning. Which meant there was a good chance the sickness wasn't real.

Had Simone's killer made the call?

Or had it not been made at all?

"Did your husband get on with Simone?"

A brief flinch. "Yes. Everyone did."

"Did he say how she sounded when she spoke to him on Tuesday morning? When she told him about the stomach bug?"

"He said she sounded weak." Natasha sighed. "I was going to go and see her on Tuesday afternoon. I got distracted. If only…"

"If you'd gone to see her on Tuesday afternoon it would have made no difference. She was dead by then."

Natasha's face fell.

"Natasha, I need to know if Simone had fallen out with someone," Lesley continued.

"Why?" Natasha asked.

"An argument was overheard on Monday night between two women."

"One of them was Simone?"

"It's a fair assumption."

Natasha's cheeks reddened. "I have no idea who would have fallen out with her. Simone got on with everybody."

Again. Simone clearly hadn't got on with everyone, or she would be alive today.

"Well if you do think of anything, call me. OK?"

"Of course."

Lesley left the house. As she walked back through the woods, she spotted a middle-aged man coming the other way. Bernard Williams.

Perfect.

Lesley stopped as she neared him. "Bernard Williams?"

"That's me."

"DCI Clarke, Dorset Police." She held up her badge. "I wonder if I might ask you a few questions."

He looked around. The shrieks of birds surrounded them. Lesley had never heard anything like it.

"Somewhere else would be better," he said. "I don't know about you, but I can't hear a thing."

Lesley didn't want to take him back to the house, where he might confer with his wife.

"Let's go to the church," she said. There was a bench outside.

Ten minutes later they were sitting on the bench. The peacock wandered off to one side, pecking at the grass, mercifully quiet.

"So," she asked Bernard, "Simone called your house to ring in sick on Tuesday morning and she spoke to you. Is that correct?"

"It is." He looked straight ahead, towards the castle.

"And how did she sound?"

He shrugged. "Weak, I suppose. I never thought she was faking it."

Lesley hadn't suggested that.

"It was definitely her that you spoke to?"

He turned to her. "Who else would it be?"

"So it *was* her?"

"Yes," he replied, looking into Lesley's face. "It was her. She told me she had a stomach bug and wasn't feeling well

155

enough to work. I said I'd pass on the message to Natasha. The conversation took one minute, if that."

"What time was this?"

"I didn't think to make a note," he said. "But I imagine it would have been around half past seven."

Lesley nodded. "And nobody called her back? Natasha didn't follow up?"

"Why would she? She had the message from me. Simone was trustworthy, there's no chance she would have lied."

His eyes were steady on her face. There was confidence in his expression, arrogance maybe.

"Tell me about your journalism," Lesley said to him. "I gather you're reporting on Simone's death."

He turned away from her to look ahead again. "I realise that's a bit awkward. What with my wife being so close to her. But I had a call from an agency, they wanted me to put together a report for the *Daily Mail*. When you're a journalist working in the modern world, you don't pass up work. It's hard enough to come by, especially when you live out here."

"You're not happy about living on the island?"

He clenched his fist in his lap. "It's fine," he said. "We have internet, I work from the cottage."

"Did you know anything about Simone arguing with anybody?"

Bernard clenched his fist tighter. "No. I barely knew the woman."

"Despite her being one of your wife's best friends?"

He turned to her. "I wouldn't say she was her best friend. Natasha was Simone's boss, you have to keep a level of professional detachment." He raised an eyebrow. "I'm sure you understand that, Detective Chief Inspector."

She met his gaze. "So Natasha and Simone *weren't* friends?"

He chuckled. "Now you're trying to twist my words. They were friendly, they weren't *best friends*, but they got on well. From what Natasha told me Simone was a nice woman, liked by everybody. Natasha certainly hadn't fallen out with her."

Lesley hadn't asked him if Natasha had fallen out with Simone.

"So you know nothing about an argument that happened on Monday night?"

He shrugged. "Sorry, I was tucked up at home on Monday night watching *Lupin*. On Netflix, we do get the twenty-first century over here."

Lesley looked at him. She didn't like this man. There was something about the cold way he'd taken the work reporting on his wife's friend's death. The way he was responding to her questions now. It made her uneasy, but that didn't make him a killer.

CHAPTER THIRTY-FIVE

Frankie opened the door to see a young uniformed police-woman with mid-length dark hair and a friendly smile.

"You need to speak to me again?" she asked.

The woman smiled and held up her ID. "My name is PC Abbott. We've had more evidence come to light, and I'm checking it with all Simone's friends."

Frankie shrugged and let the woman in. She led her into the living room where she sat down on the sofa. PC Abbott took the armchair next to her.

"What's this evidence?" Frankie asked.

"Somebody overheard an argument on Monday night between two women. I don't suppose you know who those women might have been?"

Frankie frowned. "So there's somebody who heard the argument, but they didn't know who they heard?"

"Just two women," the constable replied. "We're trying to find out if one of them might have been Simone."

Frankie looked down at her fingers. Her nails had been bitten to the quick. She turned them over in her lap and looked back at the constable.

There'd been tensions between Natasha and Simone over the last week or so. Nothing had come to the surface, nothing had been said, but Frankie had detected an atmosphere. They were skirting around something, refusing to get it into the open. Frankie had wondered if Simone might be at risk of losing her job.

She looked at the constable. "I don't know who they would be, sorry."

The constable looked down at her notebook. "Everybody we've spoken to has told us that Simone got along with all her colleagues. Would you say that was true?"

"Generally, yes," Frankie said, closing her eyes briefly. "Simone was lovely, she never had a bad word for anyone. She was the sort of person who you could rely on if you needed a favour, even at short notice. Nothing was too much trouble."

PC Abbott crossed her legs and licked her lips. She eyed Frankie. "If you don't mind me saying, that makes her sound a bit too good to be true."

Frankie tensed. "She's dead. Let's not."

The constable leaned forward. "I don't mean to be disrespectful, but there must have been *somebody* she didn't get along with."

"Well, there were some tensions between her and Natasha."

Frankie didn't like betraying Natasha. All she'd witnessed was an atmosphere, nothing specific. There'd been no arguments, no harsh words. But by saying this to the police, would she be making Natasha a potential suspect?

"But it was only tension," she added, speaking quickly. "They didn't have an argument. I never heard anything, I never saw them fall out. Simone never said anything to me, nor Natasha. I'm probably just imagining things."

"So what made you think there was an atmosphere between them?"

Frankie felt her body slump. She wished she'd never said anything.

"Look, it's probably nothing."

But if Simone's killer was going to be found, the police needed to know everything. And there was no way Natasha had killed her, so she had nothing to hide.

She sighed. "They weren't meeting each other's eye as much as they might have done. They only seemed to talk about work stuff. Nothing personal, no banter."

"Is there normally a lot of banter in your team?"

Frankie gritted her teeth. The policewoman was putting words in her mouth.

"Yes," she said, "I suppose there is. We get along well, we have fun. Four women stuck on an island together, we make the best of it."

"OK," the constable said, writing in her notebook.

Frankie wished she could read upside down.

"So did Natasha say anything to you about *why* she and Simone weren't getting along?"

"I didn't say they weren't getting along, I just said I'd witnessed some tension between them. And no, neither of them said anything to me about it."

"And you definitely didn't witness an argument on Monday night? Between Simone and someone else, or between any two women amongst your colleagues?"

Frankie dug her fingers into her thighs.

"I certainly haven't seen anything in the last week or so," she said. "We all get along here. I know people expect that with an isolated community like this, we end up tearing each other's hair out. But this isn't *Lord of the Flies*. We're professionals. We know how to conduct ourselves."

The policewoman stood up. She dug into the pocket of her jacket, making Frankie wonder how hot she was, and fished out a business card. "In case you think of anything else."

For some reason Frankie hadn't expected a police constable to carry business cards. "Of course." She took the card. *PC Abbott. Major Crimes Investigation Team.*

"Please," PC Abbott said, "if you do remember anything, no matter how small, contact me."

Frankie grunted in response. She needed to get back to work. She would go to Natasha's, check in and then find a way to lose herself in bird habitats. She closed the door behind the constable, not waiting to watch her leave.

Simone's death had cast a shadow over the island, over their team most of all. Adam was upstairs watching wall-to-wall TV news on his laptop. The volunteers had been stood down and he had nothing to do. The two of them had snapped at each other last night: he was just as tense as she was.

The sooner the police found their suspect and got off the island, the better.

She went into the kitchen. A cup of tea would calm her nerves. As she approached the kettle, her phone buzzed. She pulled it out of her pocket: a text from Anya.

I need to talk to you, it said. *It's important. Meet me outside the cafe at 7pm.*

CHAPTER THIRTY-SIX

Johnny had arrived in the office at half past nine, looking sheepish. Dennis had asked how his wife was and Johnny had shrugged in response.

"Are you sure you should be here?" Dennis said.

Johnny nodded. "Best to distract myself." He didn't meet Dennis's eye.

Now, an hour later, the three men were at their desks peering into their computer screens. Johnny and Mike were trawling through records of the people working on the island. Dennis was looking at tidal maps, trying to work out where Simone might have gone into the water in order to wash up on the beach where she'd been found. He felt a hand on his shoulder and looked up.

Johnny stood behind him, leaning over.

"Er, Sarge?" he muttered.

Johnny glanced at Mike. Mike's shoulders had tensed but he was still looking at his screen.

Dennis turned to the DC. "What's wrong, Johnny? Is it your wife?"

Johnny shook his head. "I found something weird on the system."

"What do you mean, *weird*?"

Once again, Johnny glanced across at Mike. "Can we go into the DCI's office?"

Dennis searched Johnny's face. What was this about?

He shrugged. "Very well."

He led Johnny into the office. They'd used this space a few times since the DCI had been on Brownsea Island. It was useful to have somewhere quiet away from the hum of the open-plan office.

Dennis closed the door and stood with his back to it, looking at Johnny. Johnny stood opposite him, his hand on the back of one of the chairs.

"What's the problem, Johnny?"

Johnny licked his lips and looked down at the floor.

"It's something I found on HOLMES, Sarge."

"About Simone Browning?"

Johnny looked up and met Dennis's gaze. He shook his head. "It's about the DCI. The old DCI."

Dennis took a step towards him. "Why were you looking up DCI Mackie?"

Johnny looked down again. "Sorry, Sarge. I know I'm s'posed to be working this case. But, well, you don't need to know why, but I needed to look into the details of one of his cases."

Dennis narrowed his eyes. "What cases, Johnny?" He tensed. "Is this something to do with Arthur Kelvin?"

Arthur Kelvin was a local organised crime boss. While working on the Harry Nevin murder, Dennis had discovered that he was blackmailing Johnny.

Johnny had said he'd cut all ties with the Kelvin family. But if he had, why was he looking things up on the system behind Dennis's back?

"What's going on, Johnny?" Dennis asked.

He gestured for Johnny to take a seat and looked down at him. He flicked his gaze through the glass into the office. Mike hurriedly looked away.

"Make this quick, Johnny," Dennis said. "It's Kelvin, isn't it? Why were you doing work for that man?"

Johnny took a breath. "I'm really sorry, Sarge. It was just one last thing, they wanted me to check whether Kelvin had been a suspect in Harry Nevin's murder."

"What's Kelvin got to do with that?" Dennis asked. "It was his girlfriend, Priscilla."

Johnny looked up. "I know, Sarge. It's just they wanted to know if we were looking into them."

"Of course we were looking into them," Dennis said. "I went to Kelvin's house. That's where I found you, wasn't it?"

Johnny flushed. "Sorry, Sarge. Like I say. Last job."

"Is this why you came back from the island?"

"Sarge…"

"What about your wife, Johnny? Is she really having a health scare?"

Dennis had felt sympathy for Johnny. He'd protected him. But now, he felt angry.

Johnny's eyes widened. "Please don't tell the DCI, Sarge."

Dennis leaned towards his friend. "You lied about your own wife's pregnancy to get off Brownsea Island so you could come back and work for Arthur Kelvin." He felt heat rise inside his body.

Johnny clenched his teeth. "Sorry, Sarge. They told me they'd let me go if I just checked this last thing for them."

Dennis wasn't convinced. A man like Arthur Kelvin didn't let you go just for getting a piece of information about a police investigation, and a pretty minor piece of information at that.

He sighed. "So what is it you found? This *weird* thing."

"It's a DI in the West Midlands," Johnny said.

"A DI? Who?"

"Her name's Zoe Finch, she works in Force CID in Birmingham."

"That's where the DCI used to work."

"I know."

"So why is she looking into Kelvin?"

"She wasn't looking into Kelvin, Sarge. She was looking into Mackie. She left a note on the system."

Dennis scratched his chin. "Why would a DI from the West Midlands be looking at Mackie and making notes on the file?"

"Don't know, Sarge. It was tucked away where no one would find it. Not unless they were…" Johnny looked away.

Not unless they were sniffing around for organised crime, Dennis thought. He didn't know what was worse about this. That Johnny had lied to him, or that Johnny was still working for Kelvin.

But now, Lesley seemed to have asked one of her old colleagues to investigate the death of their former DCI.

Why?

Dennis took a step back towards the door. He put a hand on the handle.

"Leave it with me, Johnny. Forget you ever saw it, yes?"

Johnny swallowed. "Yes, Sarge."

CHAPTER THIRTY-SEVEN

Yolanda Harte had gathered her staff in a large, wood-panelled room at the rear of the castle. A line of French windows looked over the gardens and the harbour beyond. Rows of seating had been laid out, but nobody was sitting. Instead, they milled around, groups clumping and separating. A hum permeated the room: speculation and worry. These people wanted to get off the island. They wanted to get as far from this murder investigation as they could.

Tough, thought Lesley.

She waited for Yolanda to introduce her and then stepped onto a low stage while the room fell quiet.

She wondered what this room was normally used for. Weddings? Corporate events? Given that the castle was reserved for John Lewis partners, it was probably the latter. This stage was probably used by local bands. It would be a good spot for a police shindig.

"My name is DCI Clarke," she said. "I'm the senior investigating officer into the murder of Simone Browning, who was found on a beach just along from here on Tuesday night. I'm assuming you all know about that."

More muttering accompanied by nods.

"We've spoken to a witness who overheard an argument between two women on Monday night, which is around the time we believe Simone was killed. But we don't know who these two women were and we want to know if any of you witnessed anything. We also want you to tell us if you saw the National Trust boat being taken out to sea late on Monday night, or early on Tuesday morning. I'll be in this room for the next hour with my two uniformed colleagues."

She pointed to two of the uniformed constables, who'd paused their task of interviewing National Trust staff and taken up positions behind small tables at the side of the room.

"If you have anything to tell us, please do so as soon as possible. I know you're all planning on leaving the island today, which is why it's all the more urgent that we speak to each of you before you leave."

More muttering, raised voices. People turned to each other, their faces full of uncertainty.

Yolanda walked past Lesley, her heels clipping on the wooden stage.

"Thank you everybody," she said over the sound of voices.

The room fell quiet.

"I understand that you're all concerned about what's happened here and I know that none of this is our fault. The police are working with the National Trust to investigate this crime and to find who committed such an atrocious act right on our doorstep. You're scared, we're all scared. But if you have anything to share with the police, please do so, and then we can all get off this island and to safety."

She turned to Lesley. "That good enough for you?"

Lesley nodded. "Thank you. So you're blaming the National Trust for all this?"

Yolanda shrugged. "It's one of their women who died, stands to reason it's one of their people who did it."

"There's no way of knowing that. How much contact was there between your staff and theirs?"

"I don't have *staff*," Yolanda said, her voice harsh. "We have *partners* here at John Lewis, and our people have very little to do with the National Trust. We keep ourselves to ourselves."

It was difficult to believe that in such a small community, there weren't bonds formed between the two teams.

Lesley looked towards the two PCs stationed behind their tables. A few people had wandered over towards them, either through curiosity or because they had something to say. PC McGuigan was talking to a man, making notes in his notepad.

Lesley threaded her way through the crowd and approached them.

"And then one of them screamed at the other and ran off," the man said.

Lesley stepped forward. "Excuse me," she said to the man. "Did you witness an argument on Monday night?"

The man turned to her. "I did," he said. "Two women. Yelling at each other, they were. I could see them from my bedroom window."

"You saw them arguing?" Lesley asked.

"Heard them as well. I opened my window, I was about to tell them to shut up, then I realised they wouldn't hear me. They were too far away and they were shouting too much. That peacock was shrieking as well, I guess they disturbed it. Poor bugger."

"Can you describe these women?" Lesley said.

"I can," he told her. "I videoed it."

Lesley felt hope fill her body for the first time since she'd started on this case.

"Have you got that video with you?" she asked him.

He nodded. "It's on my phone." He pulled the phone out of his back pocket and held it up.

"Would you email that to me please?" she asked him. "Right now."

CHAPTER THIRTY-EIGHT

"DI Finch."

"You don't know me, my name is Detective Sergeant Frampton. I work in the major crimes investigation team in Dorset Police."

There was a pause.

"Hello, DS Frampton. How can I help you?"

"I believe you used to work with my new DCI, Lesley Clarke."

"I did." DI Finch sounded wary.

"I'm hoping you can clear something up for me."

"I'll try my best."

Dennis was in Lesley's office sitting in one of the chairs opposite her desk. He hadn't gone so far as to take over her chair.

Johnny had retreated to the outer office and Mike was still at his desk. The two DCs kept glancing at each other, but Johnny was saying nothing.

"I was looking through some files on a case that we're working on down here," Dennis said to DI Finch, "And I spotted that you'd accessed them as well."

"Which files might those be?"

"The records on an Arthur Kelvin."

"Ah, yes."

"Can I ask what it was you were researching them in connection with?" Dennis asked.

He didn't want to accuse this woman of anything. He also didn't want to accuse the DCI of anything. There could be an innocent explanation for what she was doing. It could be a coincidence that this woman had worked with the DCI.

If so, it was quite a coincidence.

"Yes," she said. "We believed he might have connections to a man that we've been investigating up here, a Trevor Hamm."

Dennis had never heard of Trevor Hamm. "What kind of connections?" he asked.

"Trevor Hamm runs a particularly nasty organised crime ring up here in Birmingham. He was involved in the terror attack on New Street Station and Birmingham Airport last October. Lesley's probably told you about it."

Dennis raised an eyebrow. So this DI was on first name terms with his DCI. He wondered what their relationship had been, if they were still in contact. He suspected they were.

"That's quite a coincidence," he said.

"Yes," she replied. "You've got an organised crime boss, so have we. I'm afraid ours is a bigger bastard than yours is."

Dennis winced at the language. "I think that's for us to judge."

"Terror attacks. Multiple murder attempts. People trafficking. Does your Arthur Kelvin do that sort of thing?"

Dennis clutched his phone tighter. "Mainly money laundering and drug supply," he said.

"Exactly," she replied. "We thought that Hamm might have recruited him, got his help bringing drugs into the country via Poole Harbour. Turned out he didn't."

Dennis nodded slowly. Should he ask about DCI Mackie, or not?

No, he thought. He didn't want to draw attention to that.

"Very well," he said, "Thanks for your time."

"No problem," she replied. "If there's anything I can do to help in the future, just give me a call. Oh, and give my best to Lesley, won't you?"

"I will," he replied, his tone curt.

He hung up, still suspicious of why this woman had been looking into Kelvin and Mackie.

CHAPTER THIRTY-NINE

"Sorry to bother you, Dennis," Lesley said as he picked up the phone. "How's it going back there?"

"Oh. Er, boss…"

"Are you OK?" she asked.

"No, it's alright. I just, um…Yes, what can I do for you?"

Lesley frowned. This wasn't like Dennis. Still, he might be worried about Johnny.

"Have you heard anything from Johnny?" she asked him.

"He's here," Dennis replied. "He came in late this morning."

"How's his wife?"

"He didn't want to talk about it."

Lesley nodded. She was in the office in the café building, Gail at the opposite end of the table. It made her feel like they were the Lord and Lady of the Manor at each end of the banqueting table. Her laptop was open in front of her, the video paused onscreen.

"I'm about to send you an email," she told Dennis. "It's got a video attached. Watch it, tell me what you think."

"Yes, boss."

She hit send and waited. "You got it?"

"I have. Wait a moment."

There was the sound of movement. "Where are you?" Lesley asked.

"Just walking to my desk," he said.

So Dennis was in the office, but not at his desk. Had he taken over her own office in her absence? She looked along the table to see Gail watching her. Lesley gave her a smile. Gail had been trying to contact her team in Poole for the last half hour, but the line had been consistently engaged. They both hoped that was because they were getting closer to finding usable forensic evidence.

"Sorry, boss." Dennis's voice came down the line. "I'm in front of my screen now, with the video. Give me a moment to watch it."

"OK," Lesley said. She drummed her fingers on the desk as she waited.

"Who are these women?" Dennis asked.

"Two of Simone's colleagues," Lesley replied. "Anya Davinski and Natasha Williams."

"Which is which?"

"Anya's the short thin one with the blonde hair, Natasha's taller with dark hair."

"It's difficult to see in the dusk," Dennis replied.

"I'm hoping you can get it enhanced," she said.

At the other end of the table Gail gestured to get Lesley's attention. "You want me to make a call?" she whispered.

Lesley shook her head. Gail had enough to do and Lesley knew she wanted to be off the island as soon as possible. Dennis could handle this.

"Is this the argument that you were told about?" Dennis asked.

"It certainly is," Lesley replied. "We assumed that Simone was one of the women involved, but it seems she wasn't."

"They're very angry with each other," he said.

Lesley smiled. *Angry* wasn't the word she would have used.

"They certainly are," she told him. "I need you to get that video enhanced, see if we can get clearer sound. I want to know what those two women were arguing about. Meanwhile, I'm going to be talking to them again."

CHAPTER FORTY

Elsa took a moment to compose herself before unlocking the door to the flat. After a moment, she squared her shoulders, lifted her key to the lock and pushed the door open.

"Hello?" she called as she closed the door behind her.

"In here," came the reply.

Elsa pushed down her unease at having Lesley's daughter staying in her flat and walked into the living room. She pasted a smile on her face.

"Hi, Sharon," she said. "Have you spoken to your mum yet?"

Sharon was on the sofa facing away from Elsa, phone in hand.

"I tried to call her," she said.

"How many times?" Elsa asked, knowing she sounded like a nag. She wasn't the girl's mum and it wasn't her job to do this.

Sharon shrugged. "A couple of times. I don't think she's got a signal over there."

Elsa knew that Lesley had problems with the signal in the cottage where she was staying, but she also knew that there was a signal elsewhere on the island. Otherwise, how could Lesley conduct her investigation and keep in touch with her team back at HQ? And Elsa had managed to speak to Lesley herself.

"Try her again," Elsa said.

She walked through to the kitchen where she filled the coffeemaker and left it bubbling. When she returned to the living room, Sharon was on the phone.

Elsa watched her, waiting. After a moment, she turned away and started rearranging things on a sideboard, knowing how false her movements were.

This flat didn't have many rooms. A large open-plan living-diner, separated from the kitchen by a half wall, and then two bedrooms. It had windows front and back. There wasn't *quite* a view of the sea, although it wasn't far off. But the openness of the flat, while being so attractive to Elsa when she'd bought it, meant that she and Sharon had little privacy. Elsa had been encouraging Lesley to move in with her, but now she was beginning to rethink.

Sharon slammed her phone onto the coffee table. "She's pissed off with me."

"I'm not surprised, turning up like this. She's worried."

Sharon shrugged. "I couldn't take it anymore. Not with Julieta and that sprog of hers."

"He's not a sprog," Elsa said. "He's her son."

Julieta, Lesley's ex's new girlfriend, had a three-year-old boy. Elsa could imagine what it would be like for Sharon having to put up with an extra child in the house. The feeling of being usurped.

"You can't stay here forever," she said. "Haven't you got school?"

Sharon turned in her seat and looked at Elsa. "It's school holidays, isn't it?"

Elsa clenched her fists. On the times she'd met Sharon before, the girl had been pleasant, fun even. What was with this attitude?

"So were you on the phone to your mum just then? What did you agree with her?"

"She's coming back tonight. She was supposed to be staying on the island, but she wants to check up on me."

"She wants to know you're OK," Elsa said.

Sharon shrugged.

Elsa sighed. "Anyway, I didn't come back for long. I've still got work to do."

Sharon looked at her, her expression dazed.

Elsa had been intending to work from home. She often spread papers across the dining table over by the window, enjoying the peace and quiet compared to the office. By coming home early, she figured she could kill two birds with one stone. Catch up with a backlog of paperwork and keep an eye on Lesley's daughter. Now, she wasn't so keen on the idea. She looked at her watch.

"I'll be back by seven o'clock," she said. "What time did your mum say she'd be back?"

"About the same," Sharon replied. "She's got to organise a boat off the island with uniformed police."

"Good," Elsa said. "I'll see you later."

CHAPTER FORTY-ONE

Lesley stood up. "Right, I'm going to see Anya Davinski right now."

She strode out of the makeshift office and hurried towards Anya's house. It was a few doors up from the one that she'd been allocated, looking out to sea. She wondered if it was in a better condition than her own.

As she approached, Tina appeared from the National Trust admin building.

"Boss." Tina said, "Everything all right?"

Lesley slowed, aware that she was panting.

She shook her head. "Have you spoken to Anya Davinski yet?"

"I spoke to her about an hour ago."

"Did she say anything about the argument?"

Tina shook her head. "She told me she didn't hear anything."

"What about her meeting Simone on Monday night?"

"She said Simone left her at about nine, that she went home afterwards. So did Simone, as far as she knew."

Lesley put her hand to her forehead and looked past Tina towards the house. "She's lying."

"About what?"

"It was Anya who was in that argument on Monday night. With Natasha Williams."

"Natasha?"

179

Lesley nodded.

"What time?" Tina asked.

"Ten past nine. We've got video."

"So she didn't go home after seeing Simone."

"No," Lesley replied. "She was by the church. With Natasha."

"Did Natasha say anything about it when you spoke to her?" Tina asked.

"Not a dicky bird."

Tina looked at Lesley, waiting for instructions. Lesley thought over her conversation with Natasha.

"I didn't ask her if she argued with Simone," she said. "She didn't lie to me. Not directly."

"But Anya did," Tina pointed out. "She told me she went straight home after seeing Simone."

"She might have done that," Lesley said. "And then gone out again. But both of them are hiding something."

She chewed her lip. "OK," she continued. "I want both of us in with each of them this time. I don't want to miss anything, and I want them to understand this is serious."

"Which one first?"

Natasha would be at home with her husband. The journalist. Lesley didn't want him there while she spoke to the woman.

And Anya was closer.

"Anya first," she said. She had a feeling Anya would be more likely to open up.

"Right." Tina turned away from Lesley and made for Anya's house. She was already knocking on the door when Lesley caught up with her.

A boat was approaching, heading in towards the quay. Lesley frowned. It would be coming for the John Lewis staff.

Tina knocked again. Lesley went to the front window and peered inside. The room was empty.

"Have you seen her leave?" she asked Tina.

"I went to Frankie Quinn's house, over on the other side of the island. Anya might have left at any time."

Lesley plunged her fist into her hair. "What's Anya's job? Where will she be?"

"Habitats, apparently."

"What does that mean?"

Tina shrugged.

"OK." Lesley grabbed her phone and dialled.

"DCI Clarke, everything OK?"

"All fine, Ed," Lesley said. She didn't want to alarm him. "We're working our way through interviews, and wanted to chat to the people Simone worked most closely with again. Can you tell me where I'll find Anya Davinski if she's not at home?"

A pause. "At this time of year she'd be up in the woods on the north of the island. There's a maintenance project going on up there, creating some squirrel sanctuaries."

Squirrel sanctuaries. Lesley wouldn't know what one of those was if it hit her with an acorn. "Can you be more specific?"

"Try the area around West Lake. That's where they were working last week."

"They?"

"Anya has a team of volunteers reporting to her."

"But they've not been allowed back yet."

"Still, that's where I imagine she'll be. Is there anything I need to know about?"

"Not right now, I just want a chat with her. Thanks."

Lesley hung up. "Come on, then."

"Boss." Tina nodded and started walking. Lesley didn't envy her, yomping around this island on a hot day in her heavy uniform.

As they passed the quay, Yolanda Harte was watching the boat.

"Afternoon, Detective," she said.

"Afternoon, Ms Harte. Is this boat here to take your staff off the island?"

"It is."

"We'll need to check that only authorised people are leaving. And that no unauthorised people come onto the island."

Yolanda folded her arms. "Now why would we do that, Detective?"

Lesley had no reason to suspect that Yolanda would do anything of the sort. But she needed to keep tabs on who was coming and going. There'd been no sign yet of the journalist who'd threatened to appear, but that didn't mean she wasn't on her way.

"I'm going to get one of our uniformed constables here," she said. "He'll log people onto this boat." She watched as the boat docked. "Don't let it leave till he's done that."

Yolanda gave her a thin smile. "I can assure you we'll keep everything above board."

Lesley nodded at Tina, who spoke into her radio. "Five minutes, boss."

"His name's PC McGuigan," Lesley told Yolanda. "You can expect him in the next five minutes."

Yolanda treated her to another of her superior smiles and Lesley gestured for Tina to come with her.

CHAPTER FORTY-TWO

As Frankie approached the church, she spotted Natasha and Anya heading up from the direction of the farm buildings.

"Hi," she said, hurrying to catch the other women. "I was on my way to your house, Nat. Thought I'd check in after finishing work."

Natasha gave her a thin smile. "How are you?"

Frankie shrugged. "Oh, you know…"

Natasha put a hand on her arm. "You got time for a cuppa?"

Frankie eyed Anya, who frowned at her. "Yes."

They walked to Natasha's house in companionable silence, listening to the sounds of the island. Birds over by the waterfront, the wind rustling through the branches in the woods. Frankie loved it here.

When they arrived at the house, Natasha went ahead to unlock the door.

"Everything OK?" Frankie muttered to Anya.

Anya shook her head, glancing at Natasha who was entering the house.

"Later," she whispered. "I'll talk to you later."

Natasha stopped in the doorway and turned to them. "You two alright?" She gave Anya a wary look.

"We're fine," said Frankie.

"Well," said Anya. "Not fine." She approached Natasha. "As fine as we can be in the circumstances."

Natasha gave Anya a long look. Frankie wondered what they'd been talking about before she'd spotted them. There was an air of a conversation being unfinished.

"So, how did you get on today, Frankie?" Natasha asked as Frankie followed her into the kitchen.

Frankie took a chair and watched as Natasha filled the teapot with hot water and stirred it with a spoon. She lifted the teapot, looking at Frankie, eyebrows raised. Frankie nodded and Natasha poured her a cup of tea.

She wasn't habitually a tea drinker, but there was something in the way Natasha did this. It was a ritual, the pot of tea on the table, the tin of biscuits next to it. It felt old-fashioned and homely.

"The usual," she said. "The lake hide got some damage in the storm on Sunday night. I need volunteers to help fix it, but I've managed to do what I can on my own."

"Will it be a problem?" Natasha asked.

"Not so long as we get the volunteers back soon."

"Glad to see things getting back to normal for some people," said Anya.

Frankie looked at her. "Why? What's up with you?"

Anya shook her head. "Nothing, sorry. I'm just out of sorts."

Natasha sat down and poured herself a mug of tea. "It's good to have the two of you here." She grabbed the other two women's hands. "We need to stick together, we need to look after each other."

Frankie locked eyes with Anya. She wanted to know why Anya had texted her. Even more, she wanted to know why they couldn't talk about it in front of Natasha.

She heard the front door closing in the hall behind her. Natasha let go of Frankie and Anya's hands and plunged her own hands beneath the table. She sat upright in her chair, her right eye twitching. Frankie leaned towards her.

"You alright, Nat?"

"I'm fine."

The kitchen door opened and Bernard entered. He wore a broad smile, his eyes on his wife.

"Hello, darling."

Natasha looked up slowly and returned his gaze. Frankie watched her, wondering why she'd let go of her hand so abruptly.

Bernard strolled around the table, giving each of Frankie and Anya a smile. He reached Natasha and put his hands on her shoulders. Natasha tensed for a moment and then relaxed and leaned back, her head against Bernard's stomach. Bernard bent over and kissed his wife on the top of the head.

"Good to see you all here," he said.

He stood with his hands on Natasha's shoulders, looking between Frankie and Anya. Frankie sensed that they were expected to leave.

Natasha brought her hand out from under the table and reached up to grab Bernard's hand. She closed her eyes, her hands clasped with Bernard's.

Frankie rose slowly from her chair. She felt awkward.

"Well, I'll see you tomorrow," she said.

She caught Anya's eye and flicked her head in a beckoning gesture. Anya shook her head. Frankie stared at her for a moment, then turned and left the room.

She grabbed her coat from the hook in the hallway and opened the front door. She moved slowly, waiting for Anya to catch up, but there was no sound from the kitchen.

Was there something she was being excluded from, or was Anya just avoiding her? She'd already told her she wanted to meet later on.

Frankie stepped outside. She stopped to listen. A Dartford warbler was singing somewhere nearby. She scanned the grassland ahead but saw nothing. She forced herself to listen. It was a reassuring sound. Life went on for the wildlife they were here to protect.

She should stop worrying about Anya. She would meet her friend later, and she'd find out what was going on.

CHAPTER FORTY-THREE

Lesley and Tina arrived at a lake surrounded by forest.

"This is East Lake," Tina said. "The one Ed said she'd be at is further on."

Lesley strode on ahead, impatient. This place was huge, and they didn't know their way around nearly as well as the residents. Anybody could be hiding out here.

At last they reached the second lake. It was almost rectangular, with an island toward the other end.

"Where will she be?" Tina asked.

Lesley shrugged. She checked her watch: five fifteen. "What time does the boat go back to Poole?"

"Six."

"We'd better get a move on, then. I'll go clockwise, you go anticlockwise."

Circling the lake wasn't as easy as Lesley had hoped. There was no path, and she had to battle her way through shrubs and undergrowth. Above her, trees rose up, birds louder than she was used to in the parks she'd occasionally walked through in Birmingham.

"Bloody hell," she muttered as her skirt caught for the third time on a branch. "How does anyone work here?"

After ten minutes she spotted Tina up ahead. They'd made a full circuit.

"Any sign?" Lesley asked.

Tina shook her head. "I passed a clearing where it looked like people had been working, but there was nobody there."

"Damn." Lesley checked her watch. "OK. We both need to get on that boat. We'll talk to them in the morning, they're not going anywhere."

Tina shrugged. "Sorry, boss."

"Not your fault, PC Abbott. This is just a bloody inconvenient place to investigate a murder."

CHAPTER FORTY-FOUR

Dennis had been watching Johnny all day.

The DC startled whenever a phone rang. He kept turning to look when the door to the office opened, and he couldn't settle in his chair. When Mike had asked him if he was OK, he'd replied that he was worried about his wife. She was doing fine, apparently, just a false scare. But he insisted he was in a hurry to get home to her.

At half past five Johnny glanced up at the clock and looked at Dennis across the desks. "Sarge, can I ask a favour please?"

Dennis cocked his head. "Go on."

"It's just with my wife not being all that well and that, d'you mind if I head off?"

Dennis considered. They were in the middle of a murder inquiry. They might not be on the island dealing with the witnesses, but they were processing all the evidence that was coming in. Johnny and Mike had spent the day working through the list of National Trust members who'd visited the island on Monday, checking them against police records and making calls. And Johnny had already as good as admitted that there was nothing wrong with his wife after all.

Dennis nodded towards Lesley's office. "Can I have a quick word please, son?"

Johnny flushed. He glanced at Mike, who averted his gaze.

"Of course, Sarge," Johnny said. He followed Dennis into the office.

Dennis leaned against the DCI's desk and gestured for Johnny to close the door.

"You say you need to go home early because of your wife?" he said.

"I know it's not the best time. But it's our first baby, and that…"

Dennis gave Johnny a long, slow nod, looking into his eyes. He waited. Johnny said nothing.

"Sit down, Johnny."

Johnny took a seat, looking out towards the outer office and licking his lips. He couldn't have looked any more nervous if he'd tried.

Dennis took the other chair. He leaned forwards, his hands on his knees. He hated doing this.

"I rang your house, Johnny. This morning, when you were late in. I was worried about you, wanted to check things were OK."

Johnny's eyes widened. "Sorry, Sarge. You must have missed me."

Dennis swallowed. "I spoke to your wife, Johnny."

Johnny looked back at him. He stared into Dennis's face for a moment and then slumped in his chair. He looked down at his hands, twisting in his lap.

"I'm sorry, Sarge."

Dennis reached out and put his hand over Johnny's, making the DC stop moving them. He was trying to understand what the DC was going through. But he also knew what Johnny had promised him.

"Did you get a call?" he asked. "Yesterday, when you were on the island?"

Johnny looked up. Tears pricked his eyes. "I'm sorry, Sarge. I know I told you…"

Dennis felt his chest hollow out. He'd known Johnny for eighteen years. He'd trusted him. When he'd discovered Johnny was being blackmailed by Arthur Kelvin, he'd promised to help him get free.

It hadn't worked.

"It wasn't just about the Harry Nevin file, was it, Johnny? What else did they want you to do?" he asked.

"It was Kelvin's lawyer," Johnny said. "He wanted me to see her. Last night, after I got off the boat."

"Why?"

"She asked for the file on a burglary case in Dorchester."

"And you gave it to her?" Dennis asked.

Johnny shrank back from Dennis, pushing his hand away.

"You hate me, don't you?"

Dennis looked at him. "I don't hate you, Johnny. But I do hate what you're doing. And you already told me you were stopping. You need to stop this, you need to tell Kelvin no more."

Johnny shook his head, his gaze downwards.

"It's not as easy as that. My brother."

"I know family's important, Johnny. But this is your career on the line, your credibility. If this carries on, I'll have to tell the DCI. You'll lose your job, your pension. How's that going to be for your wife and the baby?"

Johnny looked up. He wiped his eyes and drew in a shaky breath.

"I know, Sarge. I'll tell them."

"*What* will you tell them?"

"I'll tell them I can't help them anymore."

"And what about your brother?"

"I don't know. I'll talk to him."

"Your brother broke the law, Johnny. He bought drugs from the Kelvins, yes. It's unlikely he'll go to prison, as they were for personal use. But you're breaking the law now. And what you're doing is so much worse."

"Dave's a good bloke. He didn't mean to…"

"Everybody thinks like that about their family, Johnny. But what your brother did. It's his problem, Not yours." Dennis scratched his chin. "And it's him who has to pay for it. Not you, and certainly not that baby of yours."

Johnny sniffed. "You're right, Sarge. I'm sorry."

"So are you going to be leaving early?"

A pause. Johnny closed his eyes, thinking.

"No, Sarge." He looked out at Mike in the outer office. "Let me stay in here for a minute, yeah? I'll make a call, and then I'll come out."

CHAPTER FORTY-FIVE

Lesley sat on the police boat, heading towards Poole quay. She didn't like having to leave the island. She was frustrated that she hadn't tracked down Anya Davinski or Natasha Williams before she'd left. She could feel the evidence starting to take shape in her mind, but needed to know more.

Those three women, the remaining members of Simone's team. Lesley was becoming more convinced that the three of them were hiding something from her, and that whatever that something was, it might be related to Simone's death.

But she couldn't leave Elsa in charge of her daughter, not for another night. She and Elsa weren't even living together yet. Elsa hadn't signed up to be a substitute mum for Sharon, particularly when the girl was under the influence of whatever madness had driven her to leave Birmingham late at night and head down to Bournemouth without knowing where her mum was.

Lesley huddled against the wind blowing across the harbour. It was chilly out here, no matter how warm it might be on land. The wind came in from past the Sandbanks ferry, the water pockmarked with small waves. Holidaymakers were out on the harbour, enjoying the August sunshine.

Lesley wished she could relax, maybe take some down-time to enjoy being near the coast. But what with work, and Sharon, and whatever was going on between Dennis and Johnny, she found it impossible to switch off. Lesley wasn't somebody who found it easy to relax. Never had been, never would be.

The boat neared the quay. Tina was at the front, sitting with her three uniformed colleagues. She kept glancing back at Lesley as if worried she should be sitting with her new boss. A uniformed constable, part of CID, she didn't really fit in either environment. Maybe Lesley would suggest that she go for the CID exam, become a fully-fledged Detective Constable. She was confident the woman would be good at it.

They pulled up alongside the quay and Lesley watched as the man who'd been steering the boat jumped out and secured it with ropes. The four PCs waited for her to get out first, deferring to her rank. She nodded at Tina as she climbed out of the boat.

"I'll see you in the morning, PC Abbott," she said. "What time does the boat leave?"

"Eight thirty," Tina replied.

Hopefully by then she'd have sorted out whatever Sharon's problems were, persuaded her to reconcile with Terry, and put her on a train back home.

She pulled her shoulders back and looked along the quay. She'd been driven here from HQ yesterday morning, but now she was going to Elsa's. She didn't want a squad car turning up outside, it would spook Sharon and irritate Elsa. She'd get a cab. She pulled out her phone, googling the nearest taxi rank.

CHAPTER FORTY-SIX

The atmosphere in the office was tense.

Johnny sat at his desk, not looking happy to be there. He'd emerged from the DCI's office ten minutes after finishing his conversation with Dennis. Dennis had turned to him, raising his eyebrows in a question. Johnny had nodded.

Dennis only hoped that nod meant that Johnny had been able to extricate himself from whatever was expected of him this evening, without any undue consequences.

But he would need to keep an eye on the DC, make sure he wasn't at risk. He didn't relish the thought of telling the DCI what had been happening, but it was beginning to look inevitable.

"I've got something," said Mike.

Dennis looked up. "You have?"

Johnny stood up from his chair, looking glad of the distraction. He walked round to Mike's desk, an eager smile on his face. "What have you got, Mike?"

Dennis smiled at him and joined the two of them at Mike's desk.

Mike had files onscreen that they'd been given by the National Trust. They'd been provided with visitor records, a list of members who'd visited the island on Monday, as well as personnel files. The personnel files had taken some persuasion to get hold of, but Mike had managed it in the end.

"What is it?" Dennis asked.

"It's Simone," Mike said. "She'd applied for a transfer off the island."

"When?" Dennis asked.

"A week ago," Mike said. "Here."

He zoomed in on a letter. It was handwritten. A photocopy of a letter written in scratchy biro.

Dennis squinted at it. Did they not have computers on the island, or had she not wanted to use the National Trust computers?

"Does she say why she wanted a transfer?" he asked.

"Personal reasons," Mike said. "She doesn't get any more specific than that."

"And this was a week ago?" Dennis asked.

"A week ago last Friday."

"Thirteen days," Dennis said.

"You think it's got something to do with her death?" Johnny asked.

Dennis looked at him. "It's quite a coincidence, wouldn't you think?" He turned to Mike. "Who did she send it to?"

"HR manager, a woman called Sally Farthing."

"If Simone wanted a transfer off the island," Dennis said, "there are two people she would have spoken to about it. The woman from HR, and her line manager. What's her name again?"

"Natasha Williams," Mike replied. "She lives on the island with her husband. Bernard."

"The journalist," Dennis added. "The DCI told me about him."

"Do you think there was a problem?" Johnny said. "Maybe she asked for a transfer 'cos she thought she was going to be sacked?"

Dennis shrugged. "Only one way to find out."

He checked his watch. Half past six. It was unlikely the HR manager would be there now. And the DCI had left the island, so she couldn't speak to Natasha Williams.

"Call the HR manager," he told Mike. "It's worth a shot."

Mike picked up his phone. After a few moments, he shook his head. "Voicemail. You want me to leave a message?"

"No." Dennis sighed. "We'll follow this up first thing in the morning. For now, why don't you both get off home?"

The two DCs murmured thanks.

"And Johnny," Dennis added. "Tomorrow morning you go back to Brownsea Island. You can bring the DCI up to speed."

Johnny paled. "Sarge. Surely it's Mike's turn…"

"No." Dennis wanted Johnny away from potential trouble. "You've spoken to these people already. You've got a job to finish off."

CHAPTER FORTY-SEVEN

Frankie checked her phone for the third time since arriving outside the café.

Seven thirty, half an hour after Anya had asked to meet.

She looked back towards the café. There was a gate in the side wall, which she'd come through. Anya would arrive the same way. Maybe she should go and check, in case it had been locked since she'd arrived.

Frankie walked to the gate and pushed it open. Not locked.

So where is she? It was Anya who'd set this meeting up. Anya who had been so secretive. And now it was Anya who wasn't showing up.

Frankie pursed her lips and looked out to sea. She didn't need this. She'd rather be at home with Adam, tucked up in front of the TV. Each dealing with their respective shock over what had happened to Simone.

Adam had been wonderful since it had happened. He'd let her cry into his chest last night in bed, sobbing out her frustration at not being able to express her emotions to Natasha and Anya, and her fear that there might be a killer still on the island.

She shouldn't even be here.

Adam had suggested that he come with her. But she'd reminded him that she'd lived here for eighteen months and had never felt unsafe. She wasn't about to let that change now.

She walked out through the gate, towards the admin building and the quay beyond. She looked towards the castle and back towards the quay. Anya's house was on the waterfront, looking across the harbour.

Frankie hurried towards the row of houses on the seafront, her breathing fast. She was starting to feel scared. She shouldn't have come out alone. Maybe Adam was right to say he should come with her.

Stop it. She'd knock on Anya's door. If her friend wasn't in, she'd go straight home.

She hammered on Anya's door, causing a group of seagulls on the water's edge to fly into the air.

"Anya," she called. "It's Frankie."

No answer.

Frankie moved to Anya's front window. She cupped her hands around her face and brought them up to the glass. She peered into Anya's living room.

There was no movement. No lights switched on.

She went back to the door and banged on it again.

Her friend wasn't in.

Unless…

No, she told herself. *Don't be silly.*

She ran back to the garden outside the cafe. *This is a stupid place to meet.* Why had Anya suggested it?

Anya wasn't at the café.

Frankie felt a shiver run down her back.

She should get home.

She grabbed her phone and called Anya. Voicemail.

She fired off a text.

I think I missed u. I'm going home. See you in morning. Hope everything's OK.

Frankie shoved her phone in her pocket and ran for home.

CHAPTER FORTY-EIGHT

Lesley's phone buzzed as she arrived at Elsa's flat. She checked the display. It was Zoe.

She frowned and looked up at the windows of the flat. The lights were on, but she couldn't see movement. She'd deal with this quickly, then go inside and speak to Sharon.

"Zoe," she said. "I'm in a hurry. What is it?"

"Sorry, boss," Zoe said.

"I'm not your boss anymore," Lesley snapped.

Zoe hesitated. "Are you OK?"

"Sorry." Lesley put a hand on the door to Elsa's apartment block. "Just having a difficult time with my daughter. What can I do for you?"

"I've had a call," Zoe said. "From a colleague of yours."

Lesley turned away from the building. "Which colleague?"

"DS Frampton," Zoe said.

"Dennis?" Lesley asked.

"He didn't give his first name. But are there many DS Framptons down there?"

"Only one in my team. What did he want?"

"He wanted to know why I've been looking at certain files," Zoe replied.

Shit. "Did he say which files?"

"He asked me about Arthur Kelvin. I told him we were working on a link between him and Trevor Hamm."

"Quick thinking,"

"It was a story I had ready," Zoe said. "Just in case."

Lesley moved away from the door and leaned against the wall of the apartment block. "Do you think he was suspicious of anything else?"

"No idea. But I thought you should be aware. Do you want me to leave things alone for a while?"

"I think that might be an idea," Lesley said. "At least until I'm back at the office."

"Back at the office?"

"I'm on a case that's got me stuck on Brownsea Island. I can't keep my eye on my team, it makes me uneasy."

Zoe laughed. "I don't recall you keeping much of an eye on us when you were in the West Midlands."

"That was different," Lesley told her. "I'd known you for years. I've only been with these people half a minute and I'm worried they know things they're not letting on."

"Like what?"

"Like about DCI Mackie's death. I'm convinced Dennis knows that Mackie didn't commit suicide. Gail Hansford suspects something too, she's spoken to me about it."

"Gail Hansford, she's the crime scene manager you told me about?"

"Yeah. She's good."

"Not as good as Adi Hanson, I'll bet."

Adi was one of the crime scene managers in West Midlands. He and Zoe were close.

Lesley laughed. "Nobody's as good as Adi Hanson. Well, actually, I think Gail might be better."

"Better?" Zoe sounded incredulous.

Lesley felt air on her back. The door behind her was opening, two young men coming out. She gestured for them to hold the door for her.

"I've got to go, Zoe," she said. "I need to deal with my daughter."

"Good luck with that," Zoe told her. "I sympathise."

Lesley nodded. Zoe had her own son, a couple of years older than Sharon, going to university in September. She wondered whether life would get easier when Sharon reached that age.

She let the door bang closed behind her and hurried up the stairs, shoving her phone into her pocket. At the top, she paused to gather her breath and knocked on Elsa's front door. Elsa opened almost immediately. She smiled when she saw Lesley and stepped in to give her a hug.

"I've missed you," she muttered into Lesley's ear.

Lesley leaned into Elsa, allowing her girlfriend to clutch her tightly. Peering over Elsa's shoulder, she saw Sharon hovering nervously in the hallway.

She gave her daughter a smile. "Hey, Sharon. You OK?"

Sharon shrugged.

Lesley let go of Elsa and approached her daughter. She reached out for Sharon's hand, but Sharon shook her head and turned away. She walked through to the living room and threw herself onto the sofa. Lesley caught a grimace from Elsa.

Elsa went into the kitchen, rattling around in cupboards and trying to pretend she wasn't listening. Lesley took a seat at the other end of the sofa from Sharon and looked at her daughter. Sharon looked down at the coffee table.

"So that was very enterprising of you," Lesley told Sharon. "Finding Elsa's flat when I wasn't at home in Wareham."

Sharon shrugged. "You gave me the address, remember? I had a feeling you've been here more than you were at the cottage. So I came here. Glad I did."

Sharon flicked a glance over towards Elsa. "She told me you weren't at home anyway. Stuck on some island."

Lesley nodded. "Brownsea Island. There's been a murder there, but you don't need to know about that. What happened between you and your dad?"

Sharon's jaw clenched. "I'm sick of him, Mum. I'm sick of his bloody girlfriend."

"Hey," Lesley said. "None of that language."

Sharon looked up. Her eyes were wet. "That's how *you* talk all the time."

Lesley felt tension rise in her chest. "That doesn't mean it's how you should talk."

And besides, she thought, *I try to keep that language for work and not for home.*

"So have you spoken to him since you got here?" she asked.

Sharon shook her head. "I couldn't see the point."

"You can't stay at Elsa's forever."

"Can't I go to your house in Wareham? It's the school holidays, there's no reason for me to be in Birmingham."

"I don't want you alone there while I'm on Brownsea," Lesley said.

"I can stay there, wait for you to come back. Or I can come over to the island with you if you want."

"No way," Lesley said. There was a killer on that island. "I want you to go home. Back to your dad. You're supposed to be with him at the moment. You'll be coming back down here the week after next, for a week. I've booked time off work. Plenty of time for you and me to catch up. And give you a breather, away from Julieta and her son."

"He's replacing me, Mum," Sharon said. "He's got a new family and he doesn't give a toss about me."

Lesley leaned forward. "He does, Sharon. I know he's got his own way of showing it, but he loves you. You know what your dad's like, he's almost as bad as me. Focused on his work, not very good at expressing emotion. We're a pretty dysfunctional lot, aren't we?"

Elsa placed a glass of wine in front of Lesley and a Diet Coke next to Sharon. Sharon grunted thanks and picked the glass up.

"Have you two been getting on OK?" Lesley asked. "You haven't been getting in Elsa's way?"

"We've been fine," Elsa said. "It's been nice getting to know her."

Sharon looked up at Elsa and gave her a half smile. Lesley wondered how Sharon felt about both her parents finding new partners so soon. She'd hoped that Sharon and Elsa would get along. But at the same time, she didn't expect Elsa to be a second mum to Sharon. In truth, she'd expected their relationship to play out more slowly, and for the three of them not to be thrown together like this so soon.

"I'm going to check out trains to Birmingham tomorrow morning," she said. "I want you on the first train out."

"That'll be at the crack of dawn," Sharon groaned.

"OK, maybe not the first. But I've got to get a boat back to Brownsea Island at half past eight."

"Can't you get a later one?"

"No, love. They're not running the passenger boats, there's just a police boat going over once a day. I can't miss it, I'm the SIO on the case. And we've just uncovered some important evidence that I wasn't able to follow up today."

"And you reckon that's my fault."

Lesley sighed. "I don't *reckon* it's anybody's fault, Sharon sweetheart. I just know that you need to go back and see your dad. He's worried about you. He spent Tuesday night driving around Edgbaston and Harborne trying to find your friends' houses, looking for you."

Sharon's eyes widened. "Dad did that?"

Lesley nodded. "He did, love. He worries about you. If you go back to Birmingham, I think what you've done might give him a bit of a kick. He'll pay you a bit more attention, maybe keep Julieta at arm's length for a while. Give him a chance, Sharon. Can you do that?"

Sharon pulled in a sob. "I can try."

"Good," Lesley said. She put her hand on her daughter's knee and felt the muscle tense beneath it. "That's all I ask of you."

CHAPTER FORTY-NINE

Frankie yawned as she stepped outside her house.

She'd left Adam snoring. Volunteers still weren't being allowed on the island and as he was the only one here, it meant he had no work to do. She'd rope him in to help her with the work on the hide later on. It wasn't normally his area, but he needed something to do and she needed an extra pair of hands.

Frankie stretched herself out, twisting her neck from side to side. She rotated her arms to release the tension. Standing on the path outside her house, she breathed in deeply.

The air on the island was the freshest she'd ever known, full of birdsong and the whisper of the wind through the trees. It gave her a sense of calm, like nothing she'd ever experienced.

Even with the knowledge that there was a killer on this island and her grief at losing Simone, she still loved it here.

But she'd run all the way home last night, panting like a dog when she'd slammed through the front door and banged it shut behind her. Adam had hurried through from the kitchen, his eyes wide, his face full of worry. But she'd reassured him that she was safe and hadn't passed on her worries about Anya.

Where was her friend?

She needed to go check on her. But it was just five am. People were in the habit of waking early here, but it was still too early to knock on Anya's door.

She would go down to the hide on the lagoon and watch the birds start their morning. It was her favourite way to ease herself into the long hot summer days. Enjoying the cool in the hide before it got muggy later on.

She took the long route to the hide, pacing through the woods, her footsteps light. She spotted two red squirrels running up a tree trunk ahead and stopped to watch them. They leapt from one tree to the next, blissfully unaware of their audience.

She smiled. This was what the visitors came here for.

But it was so much easier to spot the squirrels when the crowds had gone home.

At last she arrived at the hide. She took the board-walk across the lagoon, fumbling in her pockets for the key. There were only three people with these keys: her, Natasha, and Ed. She had responsibility for opening it up in the morning, and Natasha closed it at night.

She pushed open the door to the hide, enjoying the familiar creak as it opened. The hide was gloomy, still chilly from the night. She walked to the long window facing over the lagoon and put her head down on the sill. It was cool. Droplets of water hung on the wood, the morning's dew lingering.

Frankie scanned the lagoon. A flock of oystercatchers were wading on the northern edge. She watched them for a few moments, holding her breath as they dabbled in the shallows.

She moved her gaze across the surface of the water, taking in the ripples from the breeze coming off the harbour. There was something large in the middle of the lagoon, something floating.

Frankie frowned.

There hadn't been a storm lately. No logs would have been felled and blown out here.

Whatever it was, she would need to investigate. The logs disturbed birds and normally they would get a team of volunteers to clear them out of the way. Today, she could rope Adam in to help her. Hopefully Anya too.

She left the hide and walked along the boardwalk, back to land. There was a fence to one side, a locked gate in it providing access to the lagoon.

She took out her keys again and opened the gate, stepping through into a cacophony of birdsong.

Here on the lagoon, where the tourists weren't permitted, she felt at one with the wildlife. She couldn't believe she hadn't discovered this island earlier, that she hadn't come here as a child when she'd first developed a passion for birds. But she was here now, in her own version of heaven.

She edged along the side of the lagoon. The land here was unstable, damp. The object she'd seen wasn't in the centre of the lagoon as she'd thought, but floating over towards the bank in the direction of the church.

She narrowed her eyes as she approached.

It was too big to be a log.

She cocked her head.

It was…

No. Her eyes were deceiving her.

She shifted closer and felt her breath catch in her throat.

A person was lying face down in the water.

Frankie sucked in a breath and called out.

"Hello! Are you OK?"

Was someone swimming out here in the lagoon at five o'clock in the morning?

She assessed the distance between her and the person. It was shallow here, but it got deeper further out.

The figure didn't move.

Frankie felt dread crawl through her.

It wasn't a *person*. It was a *body*.

She waded into the water, the chill soaking into her legs. Her heart picked up pace as she approached the body.

She hardly dared to look at it, she hardly dared to think.

It was a woman.

She had thin straggly hair and was small, almost like a child. She wore a…

Oh my God.

Frankie stumbled in the water, almost losing her footing.

The woman wore a red scarf.

A red scarf like the one Anya owned.

CHAPTER FIFTY

Lesley jumped out of the squad car that had been sent for her and ran towards Poole quay. The police boat was there already, three figures gathered near it. One of them was Johnny, the other two were male PCs.

"Johnny," she panted. "I didn't expect to find you here."

"I got a call from dispatch," he said. "I left home soon as I heard."

"You're coming to the island with me again today?"

He nodded. "The sarge told me I should come back."

"How's your wife?"

He flushed. "She's fine. False alarm."

Lesley put a hand on Johnny's shoulder. "I'm glad to hear it, Johnny. I hope she'll be OK."

He looked down, not meeting her eye. "Thanks. She'll be fine." He looked out towards the boat. "Let's just get over there."

Lesley approached the two PCs. "Is it just you two?"

"Sergeant Dillick's on his way. And PC Abbott."

"How far away are they?"

"I'll check." One of the PCs spoke into his radio, then shook his head. "It'll be half an hour before they get here."

"One of you bring the boat back for them," Lesley said. "I want to get over there right now, we haven't got time to wait."

The PC nodded and Lesley went to the boat. She looked up as Johnny approached, his face full of fear.

"You'll be fine," she told him. "You've done it once, now you know you can do it again."

He swallowed and nodded at her. She climbed into the boat then held out a hand and helped him clamber down.

One of the PCs untied the ropes and they headed out into the harbour. They were moving faster this time, a sense of urgency propelling them through the water. Johnny clutched at the seat either side of his legs. He muttered under his breath. Lesley watched, hoping he wouldn't throw up.

When they were halfway across, she pulled out her phone and dialled Gail.

"Hello?" Gail said, her voice sleepy.

"Sorry to wake you," Lesley said. "But there's been another body found on Brownsea Island."

"What?"

"They think it's Anya Davinski."

"Isn't she one of the…?"

"She is," Lesley said.

She thought back to herself and Tina racing around the island yesterday, looking for Anya. Had she been dead all that time, or had she been with whoever had killed her?

"When can you get over here?" she asked Gail.

"I was planning on meeting Gav and Brett at the quay at eight. I thought I'd get a headstart on you. But you've beaten me to it."

"When can you get here?" Lesley repeated.

Gail lived in Swanage. She'd have to get the ferry across the mouth of the harbour. Was it even running yet?

"Give me twenty minutes to get to Shell Bay," Gail said. "I'll get Brett to take the boat over there, the ferry's not running this early. Then we'll be ten minutes, it's closer to the island than Poole quay."

"Thanks." Lesley hung up.

They were near the island now, approaching the lagoon north of the quay. Lesley could see two people standing on a narrow piece of land that separated the lagoon from the harbour. Ed Rogers and Frankie Quinn.

"Can we moor up here?" she called out to one of the constables.

"Not sure, Ma'am."

Ed waved to them as they approached. He cupped his hands to his mouth, calling out. Lesley raised her arms in a shrug.

Her phone rang, it was Ed.

"Don't bring your boat in here. Take it to the quay." His voice sounded stern.

"Why not?" Lesley asked him. "This'll make our job easier."

"No," he replied. "It's a delicate habitat. You can't disturb it."

Lesley cursed under her breath. If they pulled in at the quay, getting to the lagoon would take a good ten minutes.

"We'll need to bring a boat in closer to where you found her," she told him.

"I know," he said. "But not right by the lagoon."

She sighed. "Fair enough."

She nodded to the PC who was steering the boat.

"Go to the quay," she told him.

CHAPTER FIFTY-ONE

Anya Davinski was still floating facedown in the water when Lesley arrived. Ed stood at the edge of the lagoon, looking helpless. He turned to Lesley as she ducked through a gate in the fence separating the lagoon from the hide.

"I don't know what to do," he said. "I was going to move her, but then I thought your crime scene people might prefer it if I left her how she was."

"You did the right thing," Lesley told him.

She looked at the body floating in the lagoon. It spun clockwise, hit the edge of the water, then floated back towards the centre before repeating the same movement. The current kept bringing it back to the edge of the water, where the ground was marshy and brown. The woman's arms were out, her hair floating across the water.

Lesley hated leaving her like this, but she knew that Gail and her team needed to see the woman as she had been when she was found, not as she would be after she'd been dragged out of the water. They would need to take photos.

"Who found her?" she asked.

"Frankie Quinn. She opens up the hide in the morning. She found her about an hour and a half ago."

"She was here when we passed in the boat."

Ed nodded. "She was distraught. I sent her home."

Lesley surveyed the body. *Hurry up, Gail.*

"Can you wait here a moment, Ed?" she asked him. "I need to have a word with my DC."

Johnny looked puzzled as she led him away. They went back through the gate and stood in front of the hide. It was still early, only half past six. Nobody seemed to have been alerted to what had happened. Maybe the people who lived here had more respect than the average member of the public.

"God, I wish we'd spoken to her yesterday," she said to Johnny.

He nodded. "About the argument?"

"It was her," she said. "It was Anya and Natasha who argued."

"Not Simone?"

"No. So what did they argue about? Is that why she's dead?"

Johnny looked at her. "We got some new information yesterday too, boss."

She raised an eyebrow. "And you're telling me now?"

"Sorry."

He still looked pale. He'd walked slowly on the way from the quay, not able to stop and gather his breath this time. She knew he'd still be feeling nauseous.

"What is it, then?" she snapped.

"Simone applied for a transfer off the island, a week ago last Friday."

"Thirteen days before she died."

"Yes, boss."

"What reason did she give?"

"We don't know. Mike was looking through her personnel file, he found a letter."

"A letter?"

"Handwritten. She clearly didn't want to use the computers."

"And did she say *why* she wanted a transfer?"

"We tried to call the HR manager, but it was too late in the day. Mike'll speak to her this morning, I'm sure he'll let us know as soon as he finds out."

"You keep in touch with him," Lesley said. "I want to know the minute we get a reason for Simone requesting that transfer. If someone on this island is involved, we need to talk to them." She dug her fingers into her scalp. "It could be her killer."

"Anya's too," Johnny said.

Lesley swallowed. "We still need to speak to Natasha," she told him. "I want to know why she argued with Anya, it's even more important now. I want you to do that. I'll talk to Frankie Quinn when we're done here."

"It's still early."

"I don't care how early it is, two women are dead. Did you interview her on Wednesday?"

"Her and her husband, boss."

"Good. Go and wake her up. Get her when she's disorientated, she'll find it harder to lie to you."

"Right, boss."

Johnny turned away, then turned back towards her. "How do I get to her house from here?"

"No idea."

She hadn't been in this area of the island before. She knew they were near Frankie and Simone's houses but wasn't sure how to reach Natasha's.

"Come with me," she said. "Ask Ed for directions."

"Boss."

She stepped through the gate and walked towards the body. The sensible boots she'd bought after wading through mud on her first case in Dorset were better than her usual high heels, but they weren't wellies. She moved slowly, anxious not to join Anya in the water.

"Ed," she said. "DC Chiles needs directions."

Ed looked over at Johnny. "Where do you need to get to?"

"Natasha Williams's house."

"That's easy."

Ed pointed past Johnny and relayed a set of directions. Johnny nodded thanks and walked away.

Lesley and Ed stood in silence, gazing down at Anya. Lesley scanned the lagoon, looking for signs of disturbance. At last she heard the gate opening as Gail came through.

"Sorry it took me a while," she said. "We had to lug all our kit over here. It'd be much easier if we could put a boat in the lagoon."

"That's not possible, I'm afraid," Ed said. "It's a protected habitat."

"This is a special case," Gail told him.

"It's not just National Trust rules," he said. "It's a Site of Special Scientific Interest. It's the law."

Gail gestured towards Lesley. "But *she's* the law."

Lesley gritted her teeth. "I can't just override laws Gail, and you know it."

Gail sighed. "Yeah."

She looked out at Anya floating on the lagoon. "Poor woman. Have we confirmed identity?"

Lesley nodded. "Anya Davinski. She was a person of interest in Simone Browning's murder."

"Really?"

"She was one of two women in an argument on Monday night, around the time that Simone died. We were trying to find her yesterday, have a chat with her about what they were arguing about."

"And you didn't manage to?" Gail said.

Lesley shook her head.

"I wish I'd tried harder now. I wish I hadn't got on that boat."

She sighed. "I wish I'd stayed here last bloody night."

CHAPTER FIFTY-TWO

Frankie stared into the cup of coffee that Adam had placed in front of her. It was going cold, developing a milky skin on the top.

Her body felt heavy and her chest hollow. She couldn't get the image of Anya, face down in the lagoon, out of her head.

Adam sat next to her, his arm around her shoulders. He looked into her eyes, his face full of worry.

"You don't need to go into work today," he told her.

Frankie frowned. She hadn't thought about work, not since the moment she'd gone through that gate, not since the moment she'd looked out of the hide and spotted the object in the water. Not since the moment she'd realised it wasn't a floating log, but a body. She felt numb.

"I don't know what to do," she said.

"You don't need to do anything," he told her. "You've had a shock. Just sit here, go easy on yourself."

She swallowed. "I need to tell Natasha."

"Ed will have done that," he said. "He was there, wasn't he?"

"He was there when I left." Frankie closed her eyes. "I couldn't face the police." She rubbed her eyes and looked towards the window. "They'll be coming here, won't they? They'll want to talk to me."

"I can put them off," he said. "Tell them to wait till you're ready."

No. "They need to find whoever killed her, they need to get evidence. I might know something."

"*Do* you know something?"

She shook her head and wiped a tear from her cheek.

"I don't think I do. But I might have seen something, I suppose. Something they would make sense of but that would mean nothing to me."

"Can you remember anything?" he asked. "Any sign of how she got into the water?"

Frankie slumped in her chair. "Nothing."

When she brought the image up in her mind, the scene was blurred. Apart from the sharp centre, the body floating in the water. That was as clear as if it was right here in front of her.

"I can't remember anything," she said.

Adam squeezed her shoulders. "There you go. The police won't get anything from you now, you're not in a fit state to remember. They'll wait till you're ready, till your mind's working properly again."

She turned to him. "My mind's fine, thank you."

"You know what I mean, Frankie." He stood up and pulled at her hand. "Come on. Why don't you go back to bed? It's still early."

"I can't go back to bed," she said. "I need to speak to Natasha."

"Ed will tell Natasha. You don't need to do that."

"But what if she's at risk? First Simone, then Anya…"

"You could be at risk, Frankie love." Adam sat down. "I want you to stay here where I can keep an eye on you."

She looked at him. "Don't patronise me. I can look after myself."

"I'm sure Anya thought she could look after herself."

"What if she wasn't murdered. What if…"

Frankie couldn't imagine Anya drowning herself in the lagoon. Even if she had wanted to kill herself, Anya knew enough about the water levels to realise it was the worst possible place. Much too shallow.

And with Simone having being murdered, surely…

Frankie felt her stomach hollow out. "I need the loo."

Adam moved aside for her to stand up. "I'm here," he told her. "I'm not going anywhere."

She ignored him and ran out of the kitchen, her stomach churning.

CHAPTER FIFTY-THREE

Lesley sat in the hide, listening to voices on the other side of its wooden wall. She'd been trying to call Dennis but his number was engaged.

She turned towards the narrow window that looked over the lagoon. Gail was walking her way. Anya's body had been brought out of the water and was on the ground near the hide. Gavin stood in the water, wearing a pair of waders Ed had found for him.

Lesley dusted down her skirt and left the hide, joining Gail by the gate. "How's it going?"

Gail shrugged. "We need the pathologist here to confirm the cause of death. But I think she was dead before she went in the water."

"Why's that?"

"There's none of the classic signs of drowning. Her mouth's clean, no foaming. There's damage to the skin, but that's the immersion. Doesn't tell us how she died. And there's a deep gash on her lower arm. Her wrist might have been slit."

"She bled into the water?" Lesley asked.

"There's blood in the water, but not enough for her to have bled out, I don't think. It's difficult with the lagoon diluting it, but I think she was cut elsewhere and was dying or dead when she went into the lagoon."

"So she bled out somewhere else and then was thrown into the water?"

"Either that or the gash was inflicted post-mortem," Gail said. "It's deep, but you'd need the pathologist to tell you when it happened."

Lesley frowned. "When's Whittaker getting here?"

"Around ten."

"We can't just leave her there for two more hours."

Gail shrugged. "Sorry Lesley, but we can't move her, not till he's seen her. It's bad enough that we took her out of the water without a pathologist present. But if I'd left her until ten o'clock, it would have been five hours from when she was discovered. That would have meant water damage that could impact on the accuracy of the post-mortem."

Lesley nodded.

None of this was Gail's fault. Gail was efficient. She'd got straight in her car and arranged for her team to pick her up from Shell Bay so she didn't have to wait for the ferry. She was already doing the pathologist's job for him, as well as her own.

"So what about forensics?" Lesley asked her. "Have you got anything yet?"

"Gav and Brett are combing the area for anything the killer might have left behind. I've spoken to Uniform about getting a diver out. There's nothing yet, but it's early days."

"Are we sure there's a killer? She couldn't have inflicted this on herself?"

"Again you'd have to ask Whittaker. But I think she'd have been too weak to get herself here. And if you were going to drown yourself, you wouldn't do it in a shallow lagoon."

"Accidental?"

"Possible, but unlikely with the injury to her arm." Gail rubbed her eyes. "But I'm just a CSM. Don't take my word for it."

"Your word's what I've got right now."

Gail shrugged.

"What about damage to the undergrowth or the soil?" Lesley asked. "Was she dragged?"

"There's no sign of dragging. We think she was carried. We're looking for shoe prints. We don't think she came in on a boat or via the harbour. There's no sign of damage to the lagoon wall, and it's not the most robust."

"Somebody couldn't have pushed her over it from a boat?"

"There's a lot of ground to cover, separating the lagoon from the harbour. We're checking for damage. But based on where she was found, if I had to speculate, I'd say that whoever brought her in, came through that gate."

She nodded towards the gate they'd been using, the one next to the hide.

"It's got a padlock," Lesley said.

Gail nodded. "I've spoken to Ed Rogers, he says three people have keys to that gate. Himself, Frankie Quinn and Natasha Williams."

"Natasha Williams," Lesley said. "Johnny's on his way to interview her."

Gail shrugged. "I need to get back, I don't want to leave Gav and Brett doing all the work."

"Fine," Lesley told her. "Just let me know if you find anything, yes?"

She turned to see Johnny approaching from inland. She hurried along the path to meet him.

"How did you get on?" she asked.

"She's not there," he said.

"Not there? At eight o'clock in the morning?"

"People get up early here, that's what I've been told."

"Was her husband there?"

He nodded. "He was just about to go out, still writing his story on Simone's murder. I guess he'll be writing about Anya's now."

"Did you tell him?"

"I thought the last person who should know was a journalist."

"But his wife needs to know," Lesley said. "She was Anya's manager."

She felt her shoulders sink. Natasha had a key to the gate. And she'd argued with Anya on Monday night. Simone had requested a transfer. Was Natasha the reason for that?

"We need to speak to Natasha Williams," she said. "Urgently."

Johnny looked at her. "I don't see how, if we can't find her."

"Where does she normally work?"

"No idea, boss."

"Did she tell you anything about her work when you interviewed her the other day?"

"I just talked to her about Simone," Johnny said. "Yeah."

Lesley turned towards the lagoon. She made her way towards the spot where Anya's body lay on the ground.

Ed was walking her way. "Everything alright?" he asked, noticing the look on her face.

"No. I need to find Natasha Williams. She's not at home, where will she be?"

"She'll be in the woodland on the east side of the island," he said. "Penelope Park. That's where she normally starts the morning."

"Penelope Park?"

"It's an area of woodland. We're doing work there to provide habitats for squirrels."

Bloody stupid name, Lesley thought.

"OK," she said. "Johnny, with me."

CHAPTER FIFTY-FOUR

"Penelope Park," Lesley said to Johnny. "Where's that then?"

"It's past Natasha's house," he told her. "Over towards the viewpoint on the west side of the island."

Lesley slowed her stride to give him a smile. "Since when did you become such an expert?"

He shrugged. "I spent some time looking at maps when I was in the office yesterday. National Trust sent us detailed geological maps, tidal charts too."

"Did that tell you anything useful?" she asked him.

"The sarge worked out when it was most likely Simone was put into the water. Early hours of Tuesday morning."

"Not Monday night?"

"Low tide was at one am. As the tide rose, it would have washed things towards the shore."

"Including Simone's body."

"Yes, boss."

"So whoever pushed her in, had the boat at one am."

"Or thereabouts," Johnny replied. "Could have been a bit after."

"And it wasn't her who rang in sick."

"No."

They were passing the old farm buildings. The beach where Simone had been found was over towards the south. They took a path in that direction then turned right and walked along a wide path flanked by heathland on one side and woods on the other.

"How far?" Lesley asked.

"Fifteen minutes," Johnny replied. "The pace we're going, anyway."

She nodded. They were hurrying, almost running. She didn't want to miss Natasha Williams.

"How are you feeling now?" she asked Johnny as they walked. "You seem to have dealt with the seasickness better today."

"I think you were right, boss. Now I know I can do it, the second time wasn't quite so bad. I still felt a bit dicky when I got here though. I'm glad I didn't have any breakfast."

Lesley's stomach rumbled as if in agreement. "I'm bloody hungry," she said.

He laughed.

The last thing she'd eaten had been a Moroccan curry Elsa had cooked last night. Sharon had wolfed it down, back to her normal chatty self.

Elsa would be taking Sharon to the station this morning. Lesley felt bad about it, she'd intended taking her daughter herself before catching the boat to the island. But then she'd got the call about Anya and her plans had been thrown into disarray. Sharon hadn't even been awake when she'd left.

Would the guilt ever go away?

"How's your wife, Johnny?" she asked, remembering that Johnny was about to embark on the challenge of parenthood.

"She's much better now," he said.

She stopped walking and put her hand out to make him stop. "Was that really the reason you had to go back to the mainland? It wasn't to do with your seasickness?"

He frowned. "No boss. I had to get two more boats because of going back."

"And there wasn't any other reason?" she asked him. "Nothing to do with Dennis?"

He swallowed. He turned away from her and started walking again.

"DC Chiles," she said as she caught up with him. "I asked you a question."

"It was nothing to do with the sarge, boss," he said. "I promise."

"Is something going on between you two?" she asked him. "I thought you were best mates."

"We are," he replied, his face pale.

"So why are you barely talking to each other?"

"It's nothing," he said. "Just a silly argument about a…"

"About a what?"

He laughed nervously. "See, there you go. I can't even remember what it was about. It was a couple of weeks ago. Things'll be fine, don't worry." Johnny glanced at her. "I'm sorry, boss. I didn't realise it had got that bad." He picked up pace.

Lesley hurried to keep up, wondering if he was telling the truth.

CHAPTER FIFTY-FIVE

Natasha Williams was using a power tool to screw together two lengths of wood as Lesley and Johnny approached her. She was in a clearing in the woods, not far from the clifftop. When she spotted the two detectives she stood up, stretching her back and giving them a wary smile.

"Morning," she said. "Can I help you?"

Lesley waited until she was closer to the woman before speaking. The wood felt deserted, but you could never be sure if someone was listening.

"Have you spoken to Frankie Quinn this morning?" she asked.

"No." Natasha looked at her watch. "It's only half eight. She'll be over by the lagoon, opening up the hide."

Lesley drew in a breath. "That's what I need to talk to you about."

Natasha frowned. "Everything OK? What's wrong with Frankie?"

"Nothing," Lesley said. She looked around. There was a bench on the edge of the clearing.

"Let's sit down," she said.

Natasha gave Lesley an uneasy look and followed her to the bench. Johnny walked with them, then stood next to them as Lesley took a seat beside Natasha.

"What is it?" Natasha said. "What's happened?"

"I've got bad news, I'm afraid," Lesley told her.

"Frankie?"

"No. Anya."

"Anya? What's happened to her?"

"I'm sorry to tell you this, but she was found dead this morning."

Natasha's eyes widened. She drew back. "Anya? Dead?" She turned away. "Shit," she whispered. Her face was pale, her hands shaking.

She looked back at Lesley. "When? How?"

"She was found in the lagoon. By Frankie. It's looking like somebody killed her."

Natasha stiffened. "Again?" She closed her eyes. "God."

She opened her eyes and looked around the clearing, almost as if seeking out the killer.

"We wanted to speak to you yesterday," Lesley said, "But we didn't get the opportunity. I'm told you had an argument with Anya on Monday night."

Natasha dug her fingers into her thighs. "An argument? What kind of argument?"

"That's what I was hoping you could tell me. We have two witnesses who saw the two of you arguing."

Natasha shrugged. "I saw her on Monday night, yes. She was walking past the church when I was on my way home. I'm not sure we argued, though."

"Somebody in the John Lewis castle found it loud enough for him to video it," Johnny said.

Lesley glanced at him.

Natasha looked up at him, shaking her head. "We disagreed. I wouldn't call it an *argument*. Certainly not something you'd have heard from the castle."

That clearly wasn't true. "What did you disagree about?" Lesley asked.

"It was… personal."

Lesley leaned in. "I need to remind you, this is potentially a double murder investigation. Whatever it was you and Anya disagreed about, I need to know."

"It was about… It was about Bernard." Natasha looked down. "Anya doesn't like him. She feels uneasy having a man who doesn't work for the National Trust living here."

Lesley noted that Natasha had used the present tense. "She didn't like your husband?"

Natasha met her gaze. "She was jealous, Simone was too. Jealous of Frankie as well, most likely. They didn't like the fact that we have partners with us here. It can get lonely on the island, especially in the winter. It might look idyllic now, but you try being here when it gets dark at half past four at night, and it's freezing cold."

"So did she say anything specific about why she didn't like Bernard? Anything he'd done?"

"Of course not. It was just women being petty."

Johnny took a step forward. "Do you know why Simone requested a transfer off the island?"

"A transfer? No. When?"

"She requested a transfer just under two weeks ago," Lesley told her. "You didn't know she'd done that?"

Natasha shook her head. "It's the first I've heard of it."

"She sent a letter to HR," Johnny said. "She wanted to get away from here."

"Have you got any idea why that might be?" Lesley asked. "You were her line manager, after all."

"People move between sites all the time," Natasha said. "She probably wanted a change of scene."

"What was Simone's job here?" Lesley asked.

"Birds. She worked in the reed beds near the lagoon, this time of year. Logging species, providing data to Head Office."

"And did she enjoy that job?"

"She loved it. But that doesn't mean she couldn't have done it at another site."

"So nothing had happened between you and her that prompted her to want a transfer?"

Natasha looked into Lesley's eyes. "Nothing," she said, her voice stiff.

"You hadn't argued with Simone as well as Anya?"

"It wasn't an argument. It was just a little bit of tension, one of those things you get between friends." Natasha deflated. "Nothing to do with either of them dying."

She slumped on the bench and looked down at her fingers, still digging into her thighs.

Lesley pulled her card out of her pocket. "If you remember anything, anything at all, you will tell me, won't you?"

Natasha took the card and put it in the pocket of her fleece. She was still wearing it, despite the growing heat of the day. "Of course I will."

"Did you see Anya yesterday?" Johnny asked Natasha.

Natasha looked up at him. "She was over on the north side of the island working at the lakes. I was down here."

"So you didn't see her?"

"The last time I saw her was at the team meeting on Tuesday night."

"The one that Simone didn't make," Lesley said.

"That's the one," Natasha replied, her gaze steady on Lesley's face.

Lesley stood up. "Very well. Don't forget to call me if you think of anything. And in the meantime, we'll be having a conversation with your husband."

Natasha stood up abruptly. "Bernard? Why do you want to talk to Bernard?"

"We need to know if he saw Anya yesterday, or if he knows anything about why Simone wanted to get off the island."

"She didn't want to *get off the island*. She just wanted to move sites."

Lesley raised an eyebrow. "Either way, your husband might be able to help us."

"He's busy," Natasha said. "He's got a commission for the *Daily Mail*."

"We know," Johnny told her, his voice thin.

Lesley gave the woman a smile. "Thanks for your time."

She exchanged glances with Johnny, wondering why Natasha was so anxious about the prospect of them speaking with Bernard.

"Where can we find your husband?" Johnny asked.

"No idea," Natasha said.

"Hasn't he been hanging around near the beach?"

Natasha looked at him. She shrugged. "Not sure, you'd have to go and look."

"We will," said Lesley.

She gestured to Johnny and turned back towards the beach, questions buzzing in her head.

CHAPTER FIFTY-SIX

Tina had spent much of the morning helping Gail and her team of CSIs. They had equipment to lug back and forth between the quay and the lagoon.

They'd found a shortcut, cutting around the front of the houses on the quay. But even so, the wet ground meant they had to cut inland to reach the spot where Anya had been found.

She walked back towards the quay. There was one last trip to make, one last bag of equipment. The morning was heating up and she'd removed the jacket of her uniform. Even so, she was sweating. The nylon trousers that uniformed constables wore weren't suitable for traipsing around Brownsea Island on a day like today.

As she approached the quay, Tina spotted a boat approaching from the harbour. She stood, glad for the opportunity to take a short rest, and watched it as it closed in.

She squinted, trying to identify the people on board. Just one figure, as far as she could make out.

The boat was small, a day boat. The kind of thing you'd hire to go up and down the river. Not to come out into the harbour and travel across to Brownsea Island. It certainly wasn't one of the police boats.

Maybe it was the pathologist. Alone? Never. He'd have his assistants in tow.

The boat slowed as it passed the quay and then picked up speed. It drifted past the castle towards the beaches on the south side of the island.

Tina frowned. The National Trust had stopped any boats landing on the island. The police boat and the one used by the CSIs were right in front of her at the quay.

She ran up towards the castle, passing around its walls and skirting past the old farm buildings. If she was right, that boat was making for one of the beaches. It was the closest place you could moor a boat and it was ideal for a small craft like that.

She looked around as she ran, checking if any of her colleagues were nearby. But everyone was back at the lagoon. The only noise was the sound of the peacock shrieking over by the church.

She ran to the first beach. There were steps down, they were steep and sandy. She hurried down, panting as she went.

She stopped as she spotted the boat. It was on the beach, two people dragging it onto the sand.

Tina was sure she'd only seen one person. In which case, who was the other one? Somebody from the island?

She raised her hands to her eyes to shield them from the low sun. A woman and a man, neither of them wearing National Trust uniform.

There was gorse next to the path. She stepped to the side and huddled behind it, peering down at the beach.

The two people dragged the boat onto the sand and pushed it a few times to check it was secure. They turned to each other and spoke briefly. She couldn't make out the words.

As she watched, she realised she recognised the man.

He turned towards her. She ducked down below the shrub. As she did so, she remembered who the woman was, too.

Sadie Dawes, from the Bournemouth press. She was the one who'd called the office and told them she was coming over here.

But what was Bernard Williams doing helping her onto the island?

CHAPTER FIFTY-SEVEN

Lesley and Johnny walked towards the beach where Simone had been found on Tuesday night. The heat was picking up, only the faintest of breezes rustling through the trees around them.

They came to the beach and stood at the clifftop looking down at the sand. Gail's team had removed all their equipment, and there was no sign that this had recently been a crime scene.

Now it was the turn of the lagoon to be full of forensic equipment. Lesley hoped Whittaker had arrived by now. She needed to get back there and check his findings.

"He's not here," she said to Johnny.

He shook his head. "He could be anywhere. It's a big island."

"Let's keep looking," she said.

They turned away from the beach and walked back inland. There were a series of beaches along here, connected by paths. To reach each one you had to go inland, walk along the cliff and then follow another path down to the shore. It was tiring work. Not what Lesley had realised she was signing up for when she'd joined Dorset Police.

As they approached the next junction, she saw Tina coming the other way. She looked agitated.

"Boss!" Tina called.

Lesley and Johnny hurried to join the PC.

"What's up?" Lesley asked her.

Tina pointed down towards the next beach. "I've just seen a boat come in."

"A National Trust boat?" Lesley asked.

Tina shook her head. "A day boat, the kind of thing you'd hire to use on the river. Sadie Dawes was on it and Bernard Williams was helping her get onto the island."

"Sadie Dawes?" Johnny said. "What's she doing here?"

"Carrying out her threat," Lesley told him. "But more importantly, why's Bernard Williams helping her?"

"Fellow journalist," Johnny muttered. "All trouble-makers."

"We're looking for him," Lesley told Tina. "Show us where you saw him."

"He was down on that beach." Tina turned back the way she'd come. The beach was invisible from here, trees and shrubs hiding the path.

"Come on, then," Lesley said.

They jogged towards the path leading down to the beach. As they reached the steps, Tina ran ahead. Lesley did her best to keep up with the younger woman.

Halfway down the steps, Tina stopped. The beach ahead of them was empty.

"That makes no sense," the PC said.

Lesley came to a standstill, almost crashing into her. "There's no one here."

Tina turned to her. "They were definitely here five minutes ago."

"You sure?" Johnny said. "Have you got the right beach?"

Tina gave him a look. "Of course I've got the right bloody beach, Johnny."

Johnny smiled. "OK, calm down."

Lesley looked at Tina. "You definitely saw a woman coming in on a boat? You're sure it was Sadie Dawes?"

Tina nodded. "I know her from the telly. And Bernard Williams. I reckon he'd arranged to meet her here."

Lesley looked down towards the beach. Sure enough, there were marks on the sand. Footprints and what looked like scraping from the bottom of a boat. "So where have they gone?"

Tina ran down to the beach. She stopped at the water's edge, her hand raised to shield her eyes. "No sign of the boat."

"They've gone to another beach," Johnny said. "Maybe they heard us."

"That means she's on the island somewhere," Johnny said.

"Right." Lesley looked between Johnny and Tina. "Tina, radio your mates in uniform. The two of you, search the beaches along here. Find out where they've come in and stop them."

CHAPTER FIFTY-EIGHT

Lesley hurried away from Johnny and Tina, towards the clearing where she'd spoken to Natasha earlier. There were more beaches up here, and Natasha might know where her husband would have taken Sadie Dawes.

As she headed along the path, her phone rang. She stopped, out of breath, and pulled it out of her pocket.

"DCI Clarke," she panted.

"Lesley, it's Gail."

"Gail, how's it going? Has Whittaker arrived yet?"

"He's just got here."

"Good. What does he say?"

"Nothing yet. I'm steering well clear of him, he's in a foul mood."

Whittaker was always in a foul mood.

"Tell him to ring me when he's got a cause of death, will you?" Lesley said.

"No problem," Gail replied. "But I've got the preliminary results back on that blood we found on the boat."

Lesley turned towards the clifftop and the harbour beyond. A large sailing boat passed, looking peaceful on the water. Her breathing was heavy and uneven. She didn't like not having access to a car. Why didn't they use goddamn bikes here?

"What is it?" she asked Gail. "Have you got a match?"

"I'm afraid not," Gail replied. "It's not even human."

"What?"

"It came from a bird."

"What kind of bird?"

"Does it matter?"

"No." Lesley felt herself deflate. "Were there any more forensics on the boat? Any prints, hair strands, fibres?"

"Nothing," Gail said. "I don't think that boat was used in the crime."

"No."

Damn.

Lesley considered the boat that Tina had seen being pulled onto the beach. Was that the boat they were looking for?

"I can't come back over there right now," she told Gail. "We've had a development, we're trying to find a boat that we think has come into the island."

"A boat?"

"Long story. Tell Whittaker to ring me when he's got a cause of death, yes?"

"Of course." Gail hung up.

Lesley plunged her phone in her pocket and carried on running.

CHAPTER FIFTY-NINE

"Sally Farthing speaking. Can I help you?"

Mike glanced at his screen again, checking the hand-written note from Simone Browning that he'd found in her HR file.

"I hope so," he said. "My name is DC Legg, I'm calling from Dorset Police. I gather you're the person who provided us with Simone Browning's HR file."

"Simone Browning?"

"She worked on Brownsea Island."

"Oh. The one who was murdered?"

How could this woman have forgotten the name of a murder victim so quickly? "Yes," he said. "You gave us a copy of her file and we found a letter requesting a transfer off the island."

"Oh."

Mike wondered how many files this woman had to deal with and whether she could remember the content of any of them.

"I'm calling to find out if you know the reason that Simone requested a transfer."

"Have you spoken to her line manager?"

"Her line manager's Natasha Williams. We're trying to get hold of her, but I was also hoping to speak to somebody less closely involved."

"OK," Sally said. "I get you. Hang on a minute, I'll need to speak to my manager."

Mike rolled his eyes as the on-hold music kicked in. What was it about dealing with corporate offices? Nobody ever took responsibility, they always wanted to pass it up the line.

"Everything all right?" Dennis was looking across the desk at him.

"On hold to the National Trust HR team," Mike replied. "I don't expect I'm going to get anything useful."

"Keep trying," Dennis told him, "You never know."

Mike nodded. He leaned back in his chair, looking up at the ceiling. One of the lights was flickering, casting an eerie light show over the office.

"Hello?"

Mike sat up in his chair, almost tipping it over.

"Yes," he said. "I'm still here."

"OK." It was a different voice. "This is Rebecca Hewitt. I gather you want to know about Simone Browning."

"Yes. Did you speak to her?"

"I called her to follow up on the letter she sent us. We always conduct an interview with any staff member who requests a transfer."

"So what can you tell me?"

"To be honest, It was all a bit odd."

"Odd?"

"She told me she was scared."

"Scared of what? Was she being bullied?"

"No. I asked her about workplace harassment, and she said that wasn't the case."

"Who was she scared of? Her manager, Natasha?"

"This is confidential."

"It's a murder investigation." Mike bit down frustration.

"Yes." A pause. "She was scared of Natasha's husband."

Mike waved across the desk to get Dennis's attention.

"Did Simone tell you why she was scared of Bernard?" he asked.

"She didn't say," Rebecca replied. "She was nervous about talking about it. But reading between the lines, I got the feeling she'd confronted him about his relationship with his wife."

Mike felt himself tense. "Confronted him about what, specifically?"

"Like I say, she wouldn't go into detail. But I suggest you talk to Natasha."

CHAPTER SIXTY

Lesley spotted Johnny up ahead of her, standing at the head of one of the paths leading down to the beaches.

She picked up speed and strode towards him. He was on the phone.

He turned as he spotted her, his face flushing.

"Ah, yes," he said. "That's all fine. Yes, of course. OK, I'll speak to you tomorrow."

He hung up and gave her a tight smile.

"Everything OK?" Lesley asked him.

"That was my wife."

Lesley nodded. "Another scare?"

Johnny looked at her for just a moment longer than felt comfortable.

"Er, no. No, she's fine. She just wanted to check on me, that's all. She knows I get seasick."

"You were fine this time," Lesley said. "You told me."

He nodded, not meeting her eye. "Yeah."

"So have you found that boat yet?" she asked.

He shook his head. He looked down at his phone and then put it in his inside pocket. Lesley caught a glimpse of the screen as he did so.

Johnny straightened. "I was just about to try this path," he said. "I can't see anything from up here, but you never know."

"What about Tina?" Lesley asked. "And the other PC's?"

Johnny shrugged. "She ran off, said she was going to radio them. They've probably found the boat by now."

"Let's hope so," Lesley said. "Call Tina, make sure she reports in as soon as she finds something. I need to go to the lagoon, see what Whittaker's got to say for himself."

"OK."

Johnny gave her a sheepish look then turned away. He realised he was walking in the wrong direction, and then turned again towards the path to the beach. He hurried down it, occasionally glancing back at her over his shoulder.

Lesley watched him, her heart pounding in her ears.

She'd seen his phone screen as he'd put his phone back in his pocket. A name, the person he'd been talking to.

She couldn't remember his wife's name, but she was damn sure it wasn't *AK*.

CHAPTER SIXTY-ONE

Elsa threw herself into the car. She'd parked on double yellow lines by the entrance to the station. She'd hoped to go into the office early, run over some sensitive files. But it was half past nine and she was going to be late for her court appearance.

A traffic warden was heading towards her. She had to move.

She tossed her phone into its holder and flinched as its ringtone burst out of the car speakers. She muttered under her breath, pulling away. She could see the traffic warden in her rear-view mirror, frowning in frustration. The woman hadn't had time to put a ticket on Elsa's car.

She hit the button on her steering wheel to answer the phone.

"Elsa Short."

"Elsa, how are you?"

She knew that voice.

He rarely called her himself, preferring to let his associates do it. She knew a personal call was bad news.

"Arthur," she replied, trying to keep her voice as light as possible. "How are you?"

She pulled out on to Holdenhurst Road and heard a Cross Country train going under the bridge behind her. She hoped Sharon was on it. She hadn't been entirely happy about having to bring Sharon to the station instead of Lesley doing it, but Lesley had to attend a crime scene. This was what being in a relationship with a copper meant. It wasn't that different from being a lawyer. Particularly with the clients she'd been dealing with lately.

"Let's dispense with the pleasantries," Kelvin replied. "Where have you been the last three days?"

"Nowhere," she said.

"I find it difficult to believe you disappeared off the face of the earth."

Elsa stopped at a traffic island, cursing the traffic. She needed to get into town.

"I've been in the office," she said. "Or at home." It paid to speak plainly with the likes of Arthur Kelvin.

"I've been expecting a call from you," he said, "About the Leonard case."

Steven Leonard was an associate of Kelvin's. He'd been fined for possession with intent to supply a few months back, and had been stupid enough to get himself caught with drugs again last week. Even with a 'friendly' magistrate or judge, she'd struggle to get him out of a custodial sentence this time.

She glanced in her rear-view mirror. A BMW was right up her arse. She scowled at it and pressed on the accelerator.

"Sorry, Arthur," she said. "I was planning on looking through the paperwork this morning, making a few calls, but something came up."

"I gather that. Who's the sprog?"

She felt her chest clench. "What sprog?"

"The kid you just dropped off at Bournemouth station."

Elsa felt her skin prickle. She checked her rear-view mirror again.

That car behind her, was it Kelvin? Or one of his people?

"Nobody," she said.

Did he know she was dating a copper?

"She's cute," he said. "Sixteen, seventeen? It's not like you to go for the young ones."

Elsa's jaw clenched. *Bastard*. "She's the daughter of a friend. I was doing her mum a favour."

Kelvin grunted.

Elsa waited for him to say he knew who Sharon's mum was, but he said nothing.

Did that mean he didn't know, or that he knew and was saving the information for when it might be useful?

The BMW was gone. *Get a grip*. She was being paranoid.

"Are you following me?" she asked him.

He laughed. "When can we meet?"

She ran over the day's schedule in her head. "Six o'clock this evening."

"Very well," he told her. "Come to the house."

Elsa swallowed. She'd only met him at his house twice before. She could only hope that Lesley would still be on Brownsea Island, that she wouldn't have to account for her movements.

"Very well," she said, turning into Stafford Road, where the Magistrates Court was.

She needed to put her game face on.

"I'll see you later," he said. "Let's hope you have good news for me."

She hung up, her breathing shallow.

CHAPTER SIXTY-TWO

Frankie's body felt heavy and her mind fogged. Images of Anya's body, floating in the lagoon, kept flashing in front of her eyes.

She'd lain in bed for the last hour and a half, tugging at her memories of the last week. The police had talked about an argument between Anya and Natasha, and Natasha had been behaving oddly.

Did Natasha know more than she was letting on? Was she hiding something?

She trudged down the stairs and pushed open the door to the kitchen. Adam sat at the kitchen table, reading on his laptop. The news, no doubt. Frankie wished he would stay off it, there was nothing good in the news. Especially not now.

"I'm going for a walk," she told him.

He frowned. "D'you want me to come with you?"

"No. I need a bit of time to myself."

"You sure?" He stood up, his face full of concern.

She knew what he'd be thinking. Two women in three days, would she be the third?

Of course not. It was broad daylight, the island was full of police. Simone and Anya had both died at night. And last night, the island had been empty of police.

"I'll be fine," she told him.

She left the kitchen and grabbed her waterproof from the hook by the door. Stopping herself, she put it back. It was muggy today, it wouldn't rain. She pushed open the front door and headed out into the woods.

There was a route up to where Natasha worked that would take Frankie past the East and West Lakes, through the woodland on the west side of the island, and then down to Penelope Park. It was a twenty-minute walk, but Frankie did it in fifteen.

When she reached the clearing, Natasha was busy at work, her back to Frankie. She had earbuds in and didn't hear Frankie approach. Frankie walked up to her slowly, not wanting to startle the other woman.

When she was right behind Natasha, she hesitated, not sure what to do. She could tap her manager on the shoulder, but that would startle the life out of her.

Frankie took a few steps back, cleared her throat loudly and stamped her feet.

Natasha looked up, pulled out one of her earbuds and turned. She smiled when she saw Frankie, then the smile fell.

"I heard," she said.

Frankie looked back at her. Natasha's face was pale, her hair messed up. "About Anya?"

Natasha nodded. "I'm so sorry you had to go through that. It must have been dreadful."

"I'm trying not to think about it."

Natasha took a step towards her, her hand out. Frankie took a step back.

"What happened between you and Anya?" Frankie asked.

Natasha's eyes narrowed. "Not you as well?"

"What do you mean? Who?"

"The police." Natasha put down her tool bag and folded her arms. "They've been up here asking questions about me and Anya arguing."

"And did you?"

Natasha sighed. "I don't want to talk about it. It's…" She looked towards the centre of the island, as if expecting somebody to appear. "It's private."

"What's going on, Nat?" Frankie asked. "You've been acting strange for weeks. And why are you wearing that fleece? You're sweating, I can see it in your hair."

Natasha put her hand to her hair. "I like the fleece. It's comfy."

Frankie was wearing her own National Trust T-shirt and even that was hot. She cocked her head. "No, it's not. Take it off, show me what you're hiding."

Natasha stared back at her, her jaw clenched. "Don't tell me what to do."

Frankie stepped in and grabbed the collar of Natasha's fleece.

Natasha seized Frankie's hand. Frankie tried to tug it down. Natasha took her other hand and pushed her away. Frankie stumbled backwards, almost falling to the ground.

"Why is it so important you keep your fleece on?" she cried.

"It's up to me what I wear." Natasha turned away and picked up her tools. "I'm busy, leave me alone."

Frankie stared at her manager. For Frankie's first sixteen months in this job, Natasha had been the perfect boss. Kind, considerate. She'd left Frankie to get on with her work without interfering, but given her support when she needed it.

But for the last two months, she'd been on edge. She'd argued with Anya and there'd been an atmosphere between her and Simone.

What had they known that Frankie didn't?

"Is it Bernard?" she asked.

Natasha's head snapped round to look at Frankie. "What are you talking about?"

"Has Bernard done something? Is that what happened between you, Anya and Simone?" Frankie felt the colour drain from her face. "Has Bernard got anything to do with their deaths? Have you?"

Natasha advanced on her, her arms outstretched. "Don't be ridiculous, Frankie. You don't know what you're talking about."

Frankie stared into her manager's eyes. Natasha wasn't just her boss, she was a friend. The four of them had been a unit. And now there were just two left.

She heard a twig snap off to one side and turned.

Somebody was coming through the woods.

Frankie put her hand on Natasha's shoulder. "Did the police say they'd be coming back?"

Natasha shrugged. "I hope not."

Frankie looked again to see a figure emerging from the trees. It was a man, middle-aged with thinning hair.

A woman trailed behind him. She was younger and blonde, wearing heavy makeup. Frankie knew her face from somewhere, but she couldn't place it.

But the man, she definitely knew. The man was Bernard.

He walked towards them, his gaze flicking between Natasha and Frankie. When he reached them he put a hand on Natasha's shoulder. She stiffened.

He looked at Frankie. "I think you need to mind your own business, don't you?"

CHAPTER SIXTY-THREE

The CSI team was wading through the lagoon, looking for forensic evidence. Lesley stood on the bank, watching. Gail called out instructions, using some sort of code. They were like a well-oiled machine, the three of them. Lesley wondered if her team would ever be like that.

She turned to see Ed coming from the direction of the quay, a grim look on his face.

"Hello," he said as he stopped next to her.

Lesley gave him a tight smile. "How are your people coping?"

He shrugged. "I've spoken to all the team leaders, they're passing on the news. Nobody knows quite how to react. Some are scared, some of them are grieving. Everyone's confused."

Lesley looked out towards the CSIs in the lagoon. She'd missed Whittaker, who'd been and gone while she'd been on the other side of the island. Anya's body was gone too, the pathology team having taken her away to their lab in Poole.

"We've got a problem with a boat," she told Ed.

"Our boat?"

She shook her head. "There's a TV reporter, Sadie Dawes. She's hired a boat by the looks of it and she's on the island somewhere. Natasha Williams's husband seems to be helping her."

Ed sighed. "I always knew I'd regret letting a journalist live on the island."

"What sort of work does he normally do?"

"I thought he was a features writer, writing stuff for magazines and newspapers. I've not had many dealings with him really. He's a funny bloke."

"Funny in what way?"

"There's something about him that gives me the chills. The way he looks at his wife. He fawns over her sometimes, it's over the top."

"Shouldn't every doting husband do that?" Lesley thought of her own marriage to Terry. Neither of them had ever *fawned* over the other.

Ed screwed up his face. "He does it too much," he said. "Like he's trying to make up for something. Are you saying he's helping this TV woman get on the island?"

Lesley nodded. "We think they're here somewhere. PC Abbott saw a boat coming in and then when we went back to where she'd seen it, it was gone."

Ed turned to her. "We have to get rid of them. What kind of boat was it?"

"A day boat. Just a little thing. Tiny cabin, outboard motor."

He frowned. "I've seen a boat like that before."

"I'm sure there are plenty of boats like that in the harbour."

He shook his head. "Not over here there aren't. They tend to stay near Poole or in the River Frome."

Lesley knew the River Frome, it ran through Wareham, where her cottage was.

"So when did you see this boat?" she asked him.

He looked away from the lagoon, his gaze clouded. "Friday? Saturday? I'm not quite sure. It was out over there, going past the edge of the lagoon. Really slowly. I just assumed it was some tourists who'd got lost."

"So it's unusual to see a boat like that here?"

He nodded. "Do you think it's the same woman?"

"I doubt that a TV journalist would have access to a boat," Lesley said. "It's probably a coincidence."

"Unless it belongs to Bernard Williams."

"You've never seen it moored up on the island, have you?" Lesley asked.

"No. But he does go back and forth to the mainland. I'm sure I've seen him coming back at times when the passenger boats aren't running."

Lesley looked at Ed.

If Bernard Williams had a boat, then it might have been him that had taken Simone out into the harbour and pushed her overboard.

"I need you to come with me," she said. "We need to find him."

CHAPTER SIXTY-FOUR

Lesley grabbed her phone as she turned away from the lagoon. She dialled Tina.

"No news, boss," Tina said. "Sorry."

"You haven't found them?"

"It's a big island. We're working as fast as we can."

Lesley looked at Ed. "If you brought a boat like that onto this island, where would you hide it?"

He frowned. "Near the scout camping ground. There are some huts near the water, you could conceal a boat there."

Lesley relayed the information to Tina. "Search there," she said. "We'll join you."

She was about to ask Ed to come with her when her phone rang again. It was Dennis.

"Dennis, what have you got for me?" she snapped.

"Everything OK?" he asked.

"We might have a lead," she said. "Bernard Williams, husband of the woman who managed the two dead women."

"That fits," he said.

"Fits? How?" Lesley felt a chill run down her back.

"Mike spoke to the HR manager," Dennis said. "Apparently Simone Browning was scared of the man."

"Scared of Bernard Williams?" Lesley asked.

"Reading between the lines, she thought there was something untoward going on between him and his wife. Domestic violence, perhaps."

Lesley thought back to the times she'd seen Natasha Williams wearing that long-sleeved fleece. Was she hiding injuries?

"OK, Dennis, anything else?"

"Nothing at the moment, boss. How are things with you? How's Johnny?"

Lesley gestured for Ed to stay where he was. She walked on ahead and lowered her voice.

"Who might Johnny be ringing with the initials AK?" she asked Dennis.

There was silence at the other end of the line.

"Dennis?"

"I don't think this is the best time to talk about this."

Lesley gritted her teeth.

"That's for me to decide, Dennis. Who is this AK? Johnny told me he was talking to his wife, but I spotted the display on his phone. What's Johnny's wife called?"

"Alice," said Dennis.

"Alice Chiles," said Lesley. "So who is AK?"

"Maybe you saw it wrong, boss."

"No one programmes their wife's initials into their phone like that. Who's AK?"

Another pause. Eventually, Dennis spoke.

"Think about it," he said.

Lesley's mind was racing, her heart too. She clenched and unclenched her fists. "Just tell me Dennis, for God's sake."

"Boss, please." Dennis didn't like blasphemy.

"Sorry. Put me out of my misery, will you?"

"AK is Arthur Kelvin."

Arthur Kelvin?

Lesley clutched the phone tighter. Ed was approaching, looking uneasy.

"You're saying that Johnny was talking to him," Dennis said.

"That's what I heard," she replied.

"He told me…"

"He told you what? Did you know about this?"

"I told him to stop. He promised me."

So Johnny was in cahoots with Dorset's biggest crook, and Dennis knew about it. And neither of them had told her.

She wished she wasn't stuck on this damn island.

"He lied to you, Dennis," she said. She took a breath. She wished she was at the office, so she could look the DS in the eye. "And you lied to me."

CHAPTER SIXTY-FIVE

"I think you should leave," Bernard said to Frankie. He walked towards them, his face hard.

"Bernard, love," Natasha said. "It's OK. She's just leaving." She looked between him and the blonde woman. "Who's…?"

"Who are you?" Frankie asked, before Natasha could finish putting the same question.

The woman shrank back. "Sadie Dawes," she said. "I work for the BBC."

Frankie laughed. "The BBC? How did you get here?"

They'd banned boats from the island. How would the BBC send a journalist over?

"I brought her," Bernard said. "I've got access to a boat."

Frankie frowned. "A boat?"

He sneered at her. "You don't need to worry about it. Natasha, ignore everything she says to you."

Natasha nodded at her husband. She tugged the sleeve of her fleece.

Frankie looked at her. "You shouldn't let him talk to you like that. I've seen the way he looks at you."

Natasha shook her head. "That's not how it is," she said. "He loves me. I love him." She smiled at Bernard, who smiled back at her.

The couple advanced on each other. Bernard enfolded his wife in an embrace. She leaned into him.

Frankie had been observing the body language between Bernard and Natasha for weeks. It had changed. It had grown unnerving. He'd been too demonstrative, too doting. And Natasha tensed every time he touched her.

Even though she was in his arms now, her body was stiff. She looked scared.

Frankie stepped towards her friend. "Has he been hurting you, Nat?"

Bernard looked over Natasha's shoulder at her, his eyes full of hate.

"You fucking women. You think all men are the same. You're just jealous."

"Why would I be jealous?" Frankie asked, incredulous.

"You can see how close we are. How much we love each other. Natasha is everything to me. You need to mind your own business."

Natasha was motionless in his arms.

"Nat," Frankie said to her, steadying her voice like she was talking to a scared child. "Tell me, has he been hurting you? Did he hurt Simone and Anya? Is this why you argued with them?"

Natasha sobbed. Bernard squeezed her tighter. Natasha made a high-pitched sound.

"You're hurting her," Frankie said. "Leave her alone."

The TV woman, Sadie, walked round them. She brought her phone out of her pocket and held it up.

"You can't film this," Frankie said.

She was about to make a run for the woman when Bernard pushed Natasha away and grabbed Frankie. He had her by the wrist, his fingers digging into her skin.

Frankie cried out. She twisted her hand but he dug in harder.

Natasha screamed and slumped to the ground. Her eyes were wild. "Bernard! Stop!"

Bernard grunted and pulled Frankie towards him.

He twisted her arm in one hand and grabbed her under the chin with the other. He had her in a firm grip. Her leg had twisted beneath her. Pain pulsed through it.

She closed her eyes. She'd sprained her ankle.

Shit, she thought. Was she about to become his third victim?

CHAPTER SIXTY-SIX

Dennis stood in the DCI's office, tapping his fingers on her desk. "Pick up, pick up," he muttered as the phone rang out. On the fourth attempt, it was finally answered.

"DC Chiles," said Johnny.

"Johnny," said Dennis. "Why aren't you picking up?"

"Sarge?" Johnny replied. "What's up?"

"*You're* up," Dennis said. "You lied to me."

"I don't know what you're talking about. I'm sorry, Sarge, but I can't talk. We're looking for a guy who we think might be the killer."

"Johnny," Dennis said. "How long have you known me?"

"Eighteen years, Sarge. Look. Can we do this another—"

"And how long have you been lying to me?"

Silence.

"Johnny?"

"I told you I'd stop, Sarge. I am stopping."

"So why did the DCI overhear you on the phone to Arthur Kelvin?"

Dennis felt tension grip his chest.

If he couldn't trust Johnny, who could he trust?

He'd told Lesley that Johnny was his best DC, that he was reliable. And now, there he was, proving to her that he was a liar and fraud. A criminal at that. And Dennis was here, unable to do anything about it.

"Johnny, I have no idea what she'll do," he said. "But you need to understand that the DCI knows that you've been working with Arthur Kelvin."

"Sarge," Johnny whispered. "Why did you tell her?"

If he could have, Dennis would have reached down the phone and grabbed Johnny by the scruff of the neck.

"That's not the question, Johnny. The question is why you have continued to make contact with Kelvin, despite promising me that you would stop."

Silence again.

"Johnny?"

More silence.

"Johnny, talk to me."

The line went dead.

Dennis threw his phone down on the desk.

Outside, Mike was looking through the glass that separated the DCI's office from the main room. Dennis stared at him, fighting to control his breathing.

He grabbed his phone and went to ring Johnny again, then thought better of it.

This was a conversation that needed to happen face to face. And so was the conversation he'd need to have with the DCI.

CHAPTER SIXTY-SEVEN

Tina was frustrated.

There were five of them now, scouring the island looking for the boat. Looking for Bernard, and that journalist.

Why hadn't they found them yet?

She knew this was a big island, that it took an hour to do a circuit of the place. But even so, there were only so many beaches. And there'd been no sign of a boat.

She'd covered the area near the scout camp, checking the huts, but there was nothing there. Now she was heading into the woods past the Williams house.

She'd tried the door, but there'd been no answer. She'd go up to Penelope Park where Natasha worked. Ask her where her husband might have gone.

She was about to turn off the path when she heard a voice in the woods behind. She stopped and listened.

There it was, again. A shout.

Tina scanned the woods.

The trees were dense here and she couldn't see anything other than green.

She slowed her breathing and closed her eyes, focusing on her hearing. There was a scream. It was off to the right, in the direction of the lake where they'd gone looking for Anya.

She grabbed her radio.

"PC Abbott requesting urgent assistance."

"PS Dillick here. What's happening?"

"I heard a scream in the woods." She grabbed her mobile and opened the What3Words app. "*Words. Veal. Shell*," she snapped.

"Got it. Be with you in four minutes."

She let go of her radio and started running towards the voices.

She tried to listen as she ran, but the sound of her body crashing through the undergrowth was too loud. She waded through, trying to move quickly. Plants pulled at her legs.

She should have taken the path. It was further, but it would have been quicker.

She looked off to the left, towards the path. If she ran towards that and then took the path round, would she get there quicker? Or should she carry on going?

Carry on. She was almost there.

She heard another scream and a yell.

Two women, two voices. Then there was a shout, a man.

Tina picked up pace, thundering through the woods. Brambles clawed at her, tugging at her skin. She'd pay for this later, but she didn't care.

At last she saw them.

She stopped, her breathing heavy. Up ahead in a clearing were four people. Natasha Williams, Frankie Quinn, Bernard Williams, and that journalist woman, Sadie Dawes.

Were they all working together?

No. Bernard had hold of Frankie. He held her in front of him, his hand gripping her neck. Her eyes were wide and she kept throwing her feet out in front of her. She was trying to bring them around, to trip him up.

Tina grabbed her radio. "PC Abbott here. Assault in progress. Male suspect with female in his grasp. Two more women watching."

Were the other two women suspects, or witnesses?

Sergeant Dillick responded. "On way. Two minutes."

Tina watched the four people ahead of her. They hadn't seen her. She had to intervene.

She stepped forward and the plant life crackled around her.

Frankie turned towards her, followed by Bernard.

"Help!" Frankie called. "Get him!"

Tina didn't want to hurry in case she spooked Bernard. Even though she couldn't see one, she couldn't tell for sure if he had a weapon.

The TV reporter stood outside the group. She had her phone up. She was filming.

Bloody hell. How inhumane could you get?

"Hold it right there!" she called. "Don't move."

Bernard pushed Frankie to the ground. He turned towards Tina.

He pulled something out of his pocket. From this distance she couldn't tell what it was.

A knife?

"Don't move!" she shouted.

CHAPTER SIXTY-EIGHT

Frankie felt the wind knocked out of her as she fell to the ground.

She looked up at Natasha, who was staring between her and Bernard, her eyes full of panic.

"What did he do, Natasha?" she asked. "What's he been doing to you?"

Natasha shook her head. "Nothing."

"Shut the fuck up," Bernard told his wife. He turned to Frankie.

Frankie looked up at him. He plunged his hand into his pocket and brought out a knife. It was a Swiss Army knife, the kind of thing most people on the island carried. He flicked the blade out and waved it at her.

Frankie raised an eyebrow in contempt. "You think I'm scared of that?" She turned to Natasha. "Nat, take your bloody fleece off. Show me what he's been doing to you."

"No!" Natasha cried. "It's none of your business."

"It is my business," Frankie said. "He killed Anya and Simone, didn't he? They found out. That's why Simone wanted off the island. That's why you argued with Anya. They knew, didn't they? They confronted you about it."

Natasha was crying. "It's none of their business," she wailed. "It's none of yours, it's between me and Bernard."

Bernard was looking at his wife, chewing his lip.

Now.

In one swift move, Frankie pulled herself upright and threw out a fist. She caught Bernard on the cheek.

He reeled backwards, shocked as much as injured. Bernard wasn't a tall man and Frankie was well-built and ten years younger. Her job kept her fit. His, sitting in front of a computer and writing, didn't.

She hurried towards Natasha. "If he's been abusing you, it *is* our business. You're my friend. I care about you."

Natasha threw out her arms to stop her. Frankie stopped walking, two paces away from her friend.

Natasha looked at Bernard. "I'm sorry, love."

"Why are you sorry for him?" Frankie cried.

"How dit right there!"

Frankie turned to see the policewoman advancing on them. She crashed through the bushes. "Don't move!"

Frankie turned back towards Natasha.

She stopped breathing.

Natasha was next to Bernard. She'd grabbed the knife and was holding it out, staring at her husband. She glared at him, her eyes glinting.

"Nat!" Frankie cried. "Don't!"

Natasha glanced at her and then back at Bernard.

Bernard pushed himself up. He advanced on Natasha. "You wouldn't. I know you wouldn't."

He turned back to where Natasha's tool kit had been left on the ground. He grabbed a hammer.

"No!" Frankie cried.

Bernard lunged at Natasha, but he was too slow. She ducked below his arm and threw her arm forward. The knife went into his side.

Frankie stood up, her heart deafening in her ears. Natasha grabbed Bernard and held him as he fell to the ground.

"You've been terrorising me for months," Natasha said to him, her voice low. "You killed Anya and Simone because they knew."

"No," he gasped. "No."

"Liar!" Natasha screamed.

"Stop!" the policewoman shouted. She fumbled behind her back and brought out her baton.

Natasha leaned down over Bernard and plunged the knife further into his side.

Frankie ran for them. She grabbed Natasha.

She pulled her friend's arm away, flinging the knife into the bushes.

The policewoman was on her. "Let go of him," she said. "He's injured."

"Yes, I know he's fucking injured," Frankie panted. "But he did it, he killed them."

The policewoman looked at her. "Stand back. I need to administer first aid."

There was a crash as two more police officers ran through the bushes towards them. Frankie looked from them to their colleague, who had her hands over Bernard's wound. Blood seeped between her fingers.

"Bernard!" Natasha screamed. She lunged forward. One of the officers, a young man, grabbed her and held her back.

Natasha's face was white, her mouth open.

"Bernard. Bernard, I'm sorry."

Frankie stepped towards her friend and put her arm around her shoulders. Natasha stiffened and then sank into her.

Frankie held her as she sobbed into her chest.

CHAPTER SIXTY-NINE

Lesley was heading past the scout camp when her phone rang.

"Ma'am, it's PS Dillick. We've apprehended a suspect."

"Who?"

Lesley looked round at Ed, who was running behind her.

"Natasha Williams," said the sergeant. "She stabbed her husband."

"Say again?" Lesley almost tripped over her own feet. "Natasha?"

She looked at Ed, who frowned.

"She stabbed Bernard?" Lesley repeated.

"Yes, ma'am," PS Dillick replied. "Although according to PC Abbott, it was probably in self-defence."

"Right," Lesley said, "I'll be there as quick as I can. Where are you?"

"I'll text you the coordinates," he told her.

"Thanks."

She put her phone into the inside pocket of her jacket and turned to Ed. "We need to run."

He nodded.

She wasn't sure about bringing Ed. But if there were members of his staff involved in an attack, it might be helpful to have him there.

They ran along the path above the cliff tops on the south of the island, Lesley unsure where she was heading. She grabbed her phone from her pocket and saw a text from PS Dillick: *grapes.glee.quick.* Typing what looked like nonsense into What3Words brought up the map.

"What's the quickest way to get there?"

"Along the heathland walk," Ed said. "We'll take a right at Rough Break, and then we'll be right there."

"How long?" she asked him.

"Five minutes if we run."

Lesley pulled in a breath, unsure if she could run for five minutes. When she'd been in the West Midlands, she used a car to get everywhere. In truth, she'd spent most of her time behind a desk.

But here, things were different. She'd already lost three inches around her waist. She'd come here for rest, for respite from stress after being involved in a terror attack. She hadn't expected to get fit.

She panted as they ran, forcing herself to go on. Every muscle in her body screamed at her to stop, but she knew she couldn't. There was a crime scene ahead, an assault. She didn't know if there was another murder.

She was tempted to grab her phone and call PS Dillick for an update while she ran, but she knew that if she did that her breath would give out on her.

"How long?" she panted to Ed.

"We're two thirds of the way there."

Thank God for that. She could do this.

At last she heard voices up ahead. She scanned the woods. The undergrowth was thick, the trees dense.

"Where?" she asked Ed.

"Turn right, this path coming up."

Neither of them knew exactly where they were going. They ran blindly along the path. Lesley brought up her phone. The coordinates were off to the left.

She grabbed Ed's arm and stopped. She'd heard voices again. She peered through the woods.

"There!" she shouted.

She could see two uniforms, high-vis jackets clear through the bushes.

"I'll go first," Ed told her.

He wove a route through the bushes and brambles. Lesley followed him, glad to have someone familiar with the island to guide her. At last they stumbled out of the bushes, and came upon a scene of organised chaos.

Bernard Williams lay on the ground, covered in a thermal blanket. Tina crouched over him, PS Dillick at her side. The two other constables stood nearby. One of them had hold of Natasha, who was handcuffed. On the other side of Bernard stood Frankie Quinn and that bloody TV reporter.

"What's your name?" Lesley snapped at her.

"Sadie Dawes," the woman replied. "He helped me onto the island." She pointed at Bernard.

"I don't care how you got here," Lesley said. "You shouldn't have come."

"She was filming it!" Frankie called out.

"What?"

Lesley went to the journalist. She held out her hand. "Hand it over."

"It's news," Sadie replied.

"It's evidence, hand it over."

Sadie gave her a look of irritation. Reluctantly, she fished in her pocket and brought out her phone. She slammed it into Lesley's open palm.

"I want it back when you're finished with it."

"Perhaps," Lesley replied. It depended on what was on it. "Of course, if it turns out you were assisting a murderer, we might need to keep hold of it. For your trial."

She gave the sweetest smile she could and turned to Tina and Dillick before the woman could think of a reply. "How is he?"

"Alive," PS Dillick replied. "We need paramedics asap. I called it in."

Lesley looked over at Natasha. She stood next to PC McGuigan, her gaze down at the ground. Frankie was a few steps away from her. She, too, was looking at the ground, but kept glancing up at her friend.

What had she seen?

"We need the air ambulance," she told Dillick.

He looked up at the trees. "It'll never get through."

"It can use the open land over by Penelope Park," Ed said. "There's a spot."

"How will they know?" Lesley asked.

"They've been here before," Ed said. "There was a heart attack last year."

"OK," she said. "You talk to Sergeant Dillick, make sure they know where to come."

Lesley walked towards Bernard. He lay on the ground, muttering incomprehensibly. Tina knelt over him, her hands on his chest.

"Are you OK?" Lesley asked her.

Tina nodded. Her hair was in her face, damp with sweat.

"I'm fine. Not so sure about him though."

Lesley looked down at Bernard. "What happened?"

Tina shrugged. "There was a confrontation. I think he's the killer." She glanced over at Natasha. "He was abusing

276

his wife, and when it looked like he was going for Frankie too, Natasha finally snapped."

Lesley sank back on her heels. She looked up at Natasha.

Whatever Bernard had done, she would have to arrest his wife as well.

CHAPTER SEVENTY

Lesley looked up as Detective Superintendent Carpenter's door opened. He stood in the doorway, smiling at her.

"Lesley," he said, "Come on in."

She stood up and smoothed down the skirt of her suit. It was good to be back in the office, somewhere she wouldn't have to get muddy. Somewhere she wouldn't have to run. But this was a meeting she wasn't looking forward to.

She followed the Super into his office. He walked to the low sofa by the window and gestured for her to take the armchair next to him. A pot of coffee stood on the table.

"Would you like one?" he asked.

Lesley eyed the coffee. This was only the second time she'd been asked to sit here, the first time she'd been offered a drink. For once, he wasn't pissed off with her.

That wouldn't last long.

He poured her a coffee and gestured towards a jug of milk. She shook her head and pulled the cup towards her. She drank. It was strong, better than she'd expected.

Good enough even for Zoe Finch, she thought.

She tried to lean back and relax, but her skin was on fire. She'd come straight here this morning, not stopping off at her office, not ready to face her team just yet. What she was about to do was something she didn't want to discuss with them first. If she did, she might not have been able to go through with it.

"So," he said, "we've made two arrests, I hear?"

She cleared her throat. "Bernard Williams has confessed to killing Simone Browning and Anya Davinski. Natasha Williams is pleading self-defence."

"And the witnesses?"

"Frankie Quinn witnessed it, PC Abbott saw some of it. We think Natasha Williams's case is good. CPS are unlikely to prosecute."

"Ah," he said. "I know what the politics of these things are like. Women defending themselves against abusive husbands."

Lesley frowned. In her experience, it wasn't as straight-forward as that. "She had burn marks on her arms. Her husband smoked a cigar, he'd been putting it out on her skin."

Carpenter winced. "Not surprised she snapped after that."

"Her colleagues worked it out," Lesley said. "They confronted him, that's why he killed them."

"And this BBC reporter woman, was she in on it?"

Lesley shook her head. "He contacted her after Simone's death, thought he could make a name for himself by getting on the TV."

Carpenter grunted. "Well he's certainly made a name for himself now."

Lesley picked up her cup and took a long sip.

"I need to talk to you about my team," she said.

Carpenter raised an eyebrow. "I thought you were all getting along better?"

Lesley flinched. She hadn't realised Carpenter knew they'd had teething problems. But then, the bush telegraph in this place was more efficient than she gave it credit for. She wondered if Carpenter had spoken to Dennis directly, or if he'd just put out feelers amongst other teams.

"What's the problem?" he asked her.

Lesley placed her hands on her knees. Her palms were sweating.

She hated doing this. Dennis had explained what Johnny had told him, about being blackmailed because of his brother. Dennis had told Johnny that his brother had committed a crime and should accept the consequences. Not that Johnny should commit more crimes in order to protect him.

Lesley was trying to understand what would bring a person to do what Johnny had done. She caught glimpses of it from time to time when she tried to put herself in his shoes. Especially when she thought of his wife, and the baby on the way.

"I'd like to request a change of personnel." She looked Carpenter in the eye, making an effort not to blink.

"You would?"

"I think the team needs a bit of a shake up."

"OK."

"PC Abbott," she said. "She's doing a good job. I think without her, Natasha Williams might have killed her husband. She reacted quickly, her first aid probably saved the man's life."

"Saving the life of a murderer." Carpenter sighed. "I guess that's what we do."

Lesley swallowed. "I'd like PC Abbott to be put through the CID training. If she passes the exam, she can join my team as a DC, replacing Johnny Chiles."

"Replacing DC Chiles?" Carpenter looked surprised.

"Johnny needs broader experience. He's been in the major crimes investigation team for eight years now, he needs to broaden his CV. Possibly work in another force for a while."

"Is there a problem?" Carpenter asked. "Has DC Chiles done something wrong?"

"I just think he needs more experience."

Lesley hoped to hell this wouldn't backfire on her. She knew she should report Johnny. She knew she should tell the Super what he'd done.

But she wanted to give him another chance. And if she could wangle a transfer to another force then he'd be away from Arthur Kelvin and the temptation to continue with his corrupt activity.

And then there was Dennis. Dennis had known about Johnny, but he'd hidden it from her. Again, she should report that. But Dennis, although annoying at times, was solid, trustworthy. The kind of man who would never actively get involved in corruption. The kind of man who'd done what he could to bring it to an end, and finally, belatedly, told her about it. And he was a good DS.

"I think DC Chiles would benefit from it," she told the Super. "And I think the team would benefit from having Tina as a full member."

He put his cup down. "Very well. There's a CID course scheduled next week."

"I know."

"Good." Carpenter stood up. "Is that everything?"

"It is." Lesley stood with him.

He put out his hand and she shook it. She gave him a nervous smile. He gave her a broader smile in return.

"Well done," he said. "You're clearing up these cases faster than your predecessor did."

Lesley faltered, taken aback by the comment. For a moment she considered asking about DCI Mackie's death. She thought of the conversation she'd had with Carpenter a month earlier. *If you find anything else, you bring it straight to me.*

But this wasn't the time. She wanted to get out of here, and tell the team what was about to happen to them.

CHAPTER SEVENTY-ONE

Frankie flinched as she heard a knock on the front door of her house. Adam looked up from his computer.

The two of them were sitting together at the kitchen table. He was looking at his laptop screen again, not checking the news this time, but scrolling through Right-Move. She was staring into space.

"I'll get it," he said.

She shook her head. "It's alright."

It wouldn't be Natasha, she was on the mainland being questioned. It certainly wouldn't be Bernard, he was still in Poole hospital.

Frankie hauled herself up and dragged herself to the front door. She'd spent most of the weekend sleeping. Memories of Friday's events kept flashing through her head and she'd woken twice last night from dreams that featured blood and knives.

She opened the front door, her skin tightening. It was Ed. Frankie forced herself to breathe.

"Ed," she said. "Good to see you."

He gave her a concerned look. "How are you?"

She shrugged. "As well as can be expected, I suppose. Come in."

She pulled back from the door and let him pass her and walk through to the kitchen. She realised Ed had never been inside her house before. She hadn't had much direct contact with him, everything going through Natasha. But he'd been supportive since the attack on Friday, making it clear that nothing was too much trouble for the National Trust. That they would let her do whatever she wanted now.

She and Adam had talked late into the night on Saturday, and they'd come to their decision. She'd be surprised if Ed had an answer already.

He gave Adam a nervous smile as he stepped into the kitchen. Adam stood up. He put his hand out and Ed took it nervously. The two men shook hands, both looking as if they wished they hadn't.

"Can I get you a coffee?" Adam said.

"It's OK." Ed looked at Frankie. "I've got news. Good news."

Frankie gestured towards the table and Ed took a seat. Adam closed his laptop and sat down next to him. Frankie sat at a right angle to her partner, clutching his hand.

"They're letting us move off the island?" she asked.

Ed nodded. "I spoke to head office first thing this morning, and they were more than happy to do whatever you needed. You've been through a lot, and it was at the hands of your line manager."

Frankie shook her head. "It wasn't Nat's fault. He was controlling her."

Ed looked into her eyes. "Try not to worry about all that now."

"I can't help it," she replied. "Natasha was my friend. Why didn't I see what he was doing?"

Ed gave her an embarrassed look. As a man, he wouldn't understand. And as Natasha's line manager, he would feel awkward about the fact that he too had failed to spot any problems.

"Anyway," he said. "I've arranged the transfer you requested to the Isle of Wight. There's some work going on at the Needles, trying to attract more purple herons. I thought it would be your kind of thing."

Frankie sighed. The thought of moving filled her with heaviness. But purple herons would be a challenge. And it would get her away from here.

"Where will you live?" Ed asked her.

Adam opened up his laptop. "We're looking for places to rent. It's harder, what with there not being houses there for staff."

Ed nodded. "I'll talk to head office and see if I can arrange anything for you. There are a few properties on the Isle of Wight. We can't give you one permanently, but it might be possible as a temporary measure."

"Thanks," Frankie breathed.

Anything to get her off Brownsea, and soon. She didn't want to leave the house, couldn't face going to the lagoon, where images of Anya crowded her mind. Couldn't stomach the beaches where all she could think about was Simone's body in the darkness. And she couldn't go into the woods where Bernard had tried to strangle her.

Ed stood up and gave her a tight smile. "I'm so sorry about all this, Frankie. Anything we can do to help, just tell me. Yes?"

She nodded. There was nothing he could do, the problems weren't just practical. It would take time.

"Thanks, Ed," she said.

Adam put a hand on her shoulder. "I'll see him out. You stay here."

Frankie nodded thanks and slumped down into her chair.

CHAPTER SEVENTY-TWO

Lesley sat behind her desk, watching through the glass partition as Johnny left his own desk and walked towards her. He glanced back at Dennis, his expression nervous.

You've got a right to be bloody nervous, she thought. She'd saved his skin, not telling Carpenter what he'd done. Now he was getting a transfer, instead of a sacking.

She couldn't have done that to the baby.

He knocked on the door and looked at her. She nodded. He opened the door, entered and closed it behind him.

"Ma'am," he said. "You wanted to see me."

Lesley didn't comment on the *ma'am*.

"Sit down," she told him.

He took one of the two chairs opposite her desk, pulling it slightly back as he sat. He shuffled in the chair and looked at her.

"I owe you an apology, Ma'am. DS Frampton told me…"

She raised a hand. "I don't want your explanation, Johnny. Dennis has told me what you told him. You lied to him, you made him lie to me. I've set things up so you won't be able to work with Arthur Kelvin anymore."

He paled. "How?"

She gave him a stern look. "The superintendent has approved a secondment for you. Six months working in the Met."

"The Met?" he breathed. "How the fuck am I going to…?"

Lesley gave him a warning look. "Consider yourself lucky, Johnny. You've still got a job, you'll still get paternity leave. And most importantly, you won't be going to prison."

Johnny swallowed. They both knew what prison would be like for a corrupt police detective.

"Thank you, boss," he said.

I should bloody well think so, she thought.

"Your secondment starts in two weeks," she told him. "I know the baby hasn't come yet, but I want you to take your paternity leave now."

He nodded, his face drawn.

"Clear your desk," she said. "I don't want to see you in here again."

CHAPTER SEVENTY-THREE

Elsa was sitting at her desk when her phone rang: *AK*. She grabbed it and stood up.

"You're not supposed to call me here," she said.

He laughed. "How am I supposed to know where you are?"

She said nothing. After the conversation in her car, she realised he had more awareness of her whereabouts than she'd suspected.

On Friday night she'd gone to his house, relieved that Lesley had still been busy on Brownsea Island. He'd given her instructions for dealing with Steven Leonard's latest arrest, told her which judge she needed to speak to.

She hated doing this. She'd hoped that her firm would close down after Harry Nevin died, and she'd be set free. But no, Aurelia Cross wanted to keep things going. She wanted to remain at a distance from their shadier clients, but enjoy the money they brought in. Elsa was stuck in the middle.

She turned to the window and drew close to it. She placed her fingers on the glass, pushing so the skin of her fingertips turned white.

"What do you want?" she asked.

"Have you spoken to that judge yet?"

"I put in a call," she said. "I'm waiting for him to get back to me."

"Don't wait too long. Steve is an important part of my team."

"I don't need to know that."

She didn't need to know anything more than what was necessary for her to do her job. What would Lesley say if she ever got wind of what Elsa was doing?

She took a breath. "Is that everything?"

"No," he said. "We've lost a key asset."

She didn't know why this was relevant to her. "And?"

"He's connected to you."

She frowned, turning back towards the office and scanning the room. She'd taken over Harry's office after he died. A glass-walled box in a corner with sea views.

"Who?" she asked.

She'd had no idea that any of the staff here were working with Kelvin.

"Not one of your lawyers," he said. "A copper. DC Chiles. Do you know him?"

"No. Why should I?"

"He works for your girlfriend."

Elsa felt herself slump. So he did know about Lesley.

She closed her eyes, focusing on her breathing.

"That's got nothing to do with me," she said. "I'm your lawyer, let's keep things professional."

He laughed. "I think we've gone past that now, haven't we?"

She counted to three, breathing in and then out again.

"Arthur," she said. "Everyone is entitled to a lawyer, no matter what their activity. The work I do for you is strictly related to your legal representation."

"Calling crooked judges for me?" he said. "Do you think the Law Society would approve of that?"

She felt her throat tighten. "What do you need, Arthur?"

"I need you to find me a new recruit," he said. "If Johnny Chiles is moving to London, I need someone to replace him. And I reckon, who better than the big fish?"

"What do you mean 'big fish'?"

"DCI Clarke," he said. "She'll know everything about what's going on in that unit. You can pass information to us." He chuckled. "Pillow talk, even between you lesbos."

She bristled. "I'm not doing it." This was a step too far.

"Yes, you are," he replied. "People don't say no to me."

He hung up.

Elsa held the phone out in front of her, staring at the display. She threw it to the floor, hands shaking.

There was no way she was going to pass information from Lesley to Arthur Kelvin. If she did that, she'd lose her job. She'd lose her licence to practice law. And she'd lose her girlfriend.

But if she didn't, what else might she lose?

CHAPTER SEVENTY-FOUR

Lesley turned into her old road in Edgbaston. Terry had gone away for the weekend with Julieta and her son, and Lesley was planning to spend it with Sharon. It was a good opportunity to pack up more of her stuff and take it down to Dorset.

She pulled into the driveway and looked up at the windows. She couldn't tell if anyone was in.

She hauled herself out of the car, eyeing the empty cardboard boxes she'd brought with her, and went to the front door. She hesitated before putting her key in the lock.

The last time she'd done this, she'd walked through to the kitchen and found Julieta standing in front of the fridge.

She shook herself out. She didn't care about that now, she had Elsa. Things were settling down with Sharon and she and Terry had finally managed to have a civilised conversation earlier in the week. They'd agreed on a new routine for Sharon, to ensure she spent time with both parents.

Lesley drew in a breath and unlocked the front door.

"Hello!" she called as she closed it behind her. "Sharon, I'm home. It's Mum!"

Sharon came clattering down the stairs. She ran into Lesley's arms and gave her a hug. Lesley held onto her, taken aback. It had been years since Sharon had done this.

"That was nice," she said, holding her daughter at arm's length. "What have I done to deserve it?"

"I missed you is all."

Lesley smiled. It was nice to be missed. She'd missed Sharon too.

"How are things?" she asked. "Are you getting on better with your dad?"

A shrug. "I s'pose so. He's changed his arrangements with Julieta, she's not going to be here every night. It means we get some time just him and me."

"That's good." Lesley put a hand on Sharon's shoulder. "That's what you need."

Sharon nodded. "Yeah. I think I can put up with Sammy in small doses."

"Julieta's kid?" Lesley realised she hadn't known his name until now. "I'm sure he's not all that bad."

Sharon pulled a face. "He's three mum, of course he's *all that bad*."

Lesley laughed and walked through to the kitchen. It was sparkling, clean as a pin.

She wondered who'd done that, Terry or Julieta. She didn't like the idea of him taking up with a woman who cleaned her house.

But then, it wasn't going to be her house for long. They'd agreed that he would buy her out, stay here with Sharon while she decided where she was going to live. This place had too many memories, and Lesley needed a fresh start. In four months' time she'd be finishing her secondment to Dorset and would have to decide whether to stay with Elsa or come back to Birmingham.

She opened the fridge to find milk along with fresh vegetables and what looked like home-cooked meals in plastic tubs. Lesley raised an eyebrow and turned to Sharon who was standing behind her.

"Who made these?"

Sharon blushed. "Julieta did. I helped her."

"That's good."

Sharon had never cooked with her, but then Lesley had never asked her to.

"You and I can do some cooking this weekend if you like?"

Sharon nodded. "Let's bake a cake."

Lesley laughed. "We'll make some scones, have a cream tea like we did when we first got to Corfe."

Sharon grimaced. "As long as nobody gets murdered."

Lesley stroked her daughter's hair. It needed cutting. "I don't think they will, not this time."

Lesley's phone rang.

"DCI Clarke."

"Lesley, I heard you were in Birmingham."

"Hello, Zoe. You heard right. What can I do for you?"

"We need to talk," Zoe said. "About your predecessor and your DS."

"Dennis?" Lesley asked.

"Can we meet for a drink later on?"

"Of course." Lesley looked at Sharon. "Second thoughts," she said to Zoe. "You come here, have a drink with me and Sharon. Bring Nicholas if you want."

Sharon grimaced. She wasn't a kid, didn't need to hang out with her mum's friend's son.

"It's OK," said Zoe. "Nicholas is out tonight. But I'll take you up on that drink. Seven o'clock?"

It was a sunny afternoon, and would morph into a sunny evening. They could sit in the garden. "See you then," Lesley said.

Three hours later Zoe was sitting at Lesley's kitchen table, watching as Lesley heated up a meal that Sharon had brought out of the fridge. It was lasagne, one that Sharon had apparently done most of the work for. Lesley preferred that, not liking the idea of eating food that Julieta had cooked.

She scooped out three portions and placed plates in front of Zoe and Sharon and then one for herself. Behind her, rain battered at the kitchen window. So much for sitting in the garden.

Lesley poured a glass of red wine and offered Zoe one. Zoe shook her head.

"Sorry," Lesley said. "I forgot you don't drink. Hang on."

She went into the fridge and checked the shelf in the door. "Have we got any non-alcoholic stuff?" she asked Sharon.

"I'm fine with a glass of water," Zoe said.

"It's OK," Lesley replied. "I'm sure we've got something better than that."

She landed on a can of kombucha. "Oh. Fancy." She lifted it up, looking at Sharon. "Is this yours?"

Sharon nodded. "I thought I'd give it a try."

"Do you mind if Zoe has some?"

"No. I'll have one as well, please."

Lesley took two cans out of the fridge and placed them in front of Sharon and Zoe. She sat down and started to eat.

"So," she said to Zoe after a few mouthfuls. "What was it you needed to talk to me about?"

"I had a call from your DS," Zoe said.

"He saw that you'd been sniffing around the Mackie file."

"Yes," Zoe said. "But then I found evidence that somebody else has been downloading files in recent days."

Lesley looked at her. "Somebody else here?"

"Somebody in Dorset. I figured it was legit, but I thought I'd run it past you just in case. You've been working on that Brownsea Island case, haven't you? Not on anything to do with Mackie?"

"The Mackie case was closed, coroner pronounced it death by suicide." Nobody should be accessing those files.

Zoe nodded. "You've definitely got somebody in your team who doesn't think that."

"Who?" Lesley asked.

"I couldn't tell, it's just a Dorset Police stamp."

Lesley frowned at her. "Are you sure?"

Zoe nodded. "If I knew who it was, I'd tell you. But somebody has been on HOLMES, checking where Mackie was found, looking through the forensics."

Lesley stared at her.

Who in Dorset Police had been investigating Mackie's death?

She'd been considering doing so herself, but she'd been so busy with her own workload that it had been put on the back burner. She knew that Carpenter took an interest, but also that he wanted to keep himself at arm's length from it.

So who? Dennis? Johnny?

"Thanks for telling me," she told Zoe. "I'll follow it up."

Zoe nodded. "No problem. This lasagne is good, well done Sharon."

Sharon grinned. "I try my best."

CHAPTER SEVENTY-FIVE

Lesley unloaded the last of her boxes into her cottage. She wasn't quite sure why she'd bothered bringing all this stuff here. After all, she was spending most of her time at Elsa's. But she preferred to have it with her than up in Birmingham with Terry.

Most of the boxes were full of books. There were a few CDs, some ornaments, a couple of photo albums, things that she hadn't thought urgent enough to bring down for six months. But now, she wasn't sure if she'd go back after six months.

Every time she considered October, when her secondment would end, it felt like a brick wall in front of her. She couldn't see past it. Couldn't see where she'd work, where she'd live.

Frank Dawson was happy acting up as DCI back in West Midlands Force CID. But Carpenter didn't expect her to stay here for more than six months. And who did she want to be with more: Elsa or Sharon?

Her daughter had to come first.

Lesley slammed the car door shut and hauled the last box into the house. She was about to close the door behind her when she spotted movement behind her. Elsa was walking towards the house. She carried a large bunch of delphiniums.

Lesley smiled. "Are those for me?"

"Nah," Elsa said. "I thought I'd give them to your next door neighbour. Commiseration prize for living so close to you."

"Oi," Lesley told her. "Don't be cheeky."

Elsa grinned and gave Lesley a kiss on the cheek. "How about a drink? I'm not working in the Duke of Wellington tonight, but we could go there."

Lesley screwed up her nose. "You really want to drink in the pub where you work?"

Elsa shrugged. "Best pub in Wareham."

"Is it?"

The Duke of Wellington was fine, but it was an old-fashioned pub that smelt of beer and sometimes sweat.

"Let's go to the Kings Arms," she said. "We can sit outside in their beer garden."

It was another sweltering evening. The heat would keep up through the night, and Lesley would be roasted alive in the eaves bedroom of her cottage.

"Fair enough," said Elsa. "What d'you want to do with these flowers?"

Lesley put the box of books down on the coffee table and took the flowers from Elsa. "I'm sure I've got a vase somewhere."

She looked down at the boxes. There was a vase in one of them, but she had no idea which.

Elsa was grinning, her eyes glinting.

"OK," Lesley said. "I'll put them in a pint glass."

"Sophisticated, aren't you?" Elsa laughed.

Lesley gave her a mock punch on the arm.

Ten minutes later the flowers were safely in the sink, and Lesley and Elsa were in the beer garden of the Kings Arms. Lesley had a gin and tonic in front of her and Elsa a glass of red wine.

Lesley sipped at her drink and leaned back, feeling the evening sun on her face.

"I could get used to this," she said.

"So do," Elsa told her.

Lesley opened her eyes and looked at her girlfriend. "You do know I've got to go back to Birmingham in four months?"

Elsa's face darkened. "Let's not discuss that."

Lesley looked into Elsa's eyes. She knew that at some point they would have to talk about this.

"You wanted to leave your firm," she said.

Elsa shrugged. "Looks like that's not going to happen."

"No?"

Elsa shook her head. Her body had slumped and her face hardened. "Let's not talk about work."

"OK." Lesley grabbed Elsa's hand and squeezed it. "Let's enjoy the evening."

Elsa raised a glass. Lesley held hers up to it.

"Here's to you being in Dorset for as long as possible," Elsa said.

Lesley smiled. "I'll drink to that."

I hope you enjoyed *The Island Murders*. Do you want to know more about DCI Mackie's death? The prequel novella, *The Ballard Down Murder*, is free from my book club at rachelmclean.com/ballard.

Thanks,

Rachel McLean